D1535406

# SWEET STARLIGHT

KAY CORRELL

ROSE QUARTZ PRESS

Published by Rose Quartz Press

050618

*This book is dedicated to the wonderful writer friends I've come to know and admire on my journey to becoming an author.*

INDIGO BAY

*A multi-author sweet romance series. All of the books can be read in any order. Enjoy visiting the charming town of Indigo Bay, South Carolina.*

A complete list of the series can be found at sweetreadbooks.com/indigo-bay

NOVELS - 2018
   Sweet Saturdays - Pamela Kelley
   Sweet Beginnings - Melissa McClone
   Sweet Starlight - Kay Correll
   Sweet Forgiveness - Jean Oram
   Sweet Reunion - Stacy Claflin
   Sweet Entanglement - Jean C. Gordon

HOLIDAY SHORT STORIES - December 2017
   Sweet Holiday Memories - Kay Correll
   Sweet Holiday Wish - Melissa McClone

Sweet Holiday Surprises - Jean Oram
Sweet Holiday Traditions - Danielle Stewart

NOVELS - Summer 2017
Sweet Dreams - Stacy Claflin
Sweet Matchmaker - Jean Oram
Sweet Sunrise - Kay Correll
Sweet Illusions - Jeanette Lewis
Sweet Regrets - Jennifer Peel
Sweet Rendezvous - Danielle Stewart

Wish Upon a Shell - Book One
Wedding on the Beach - Book Two
Love at the Lighthouse - Book Three
Cottage near the Point - Book Four
Return to the Island - Book Five

**INDIGO BAY** ~ A multi-author sweet romance series
Sweet Sunrise - Book Three
Sweet Holiday Memories - A short holiday story
Sweet Starlight - Book Nine

Sign up for my newsletter at my website *kaycorrell.com* to make sure you don't miss any new releases or sales.

## CHAPTER 1

Richard Nicholson swiped the sunglasses from the top of his head and settled them on his face. He grabbed a baseball cap from the dash of the rental car and pulled it over his short brown hair. With a quick look in the rearview mirror, he figured this was as good as it was going to get.

He swung open the door and eased his way out of the flashy red sports car. He should have rented something less conspicuous but hadn't been able to help himself. A weakness of his—flashy sports cars. He clicked the button on the key fob to lock the car. The fresh, salty sea breeze was a welcome change from the hazy, smoggy air in California. It had taken him hours and hours, plus a plane change, to fly all the way across the country to reach Charleston where he'd rented the car to drive out to Indigo Bay.

He looked up and down the street, taking in the view of quaint shops and a handful of tourists browsing the storefronts. He scowled at his task, but determination swept through him to conquer the job. Why his sister had given *him* the job of finding a gift for their grandmother's birthday was a mystery to him, but he wasn't going to fail.

He was going to find his grandmother the perfect gift. Even if he hated to shop. Even if he freely admitted he was a horrible gift-giver and usually just called his assistant to pick out something for him. But it didn't seem right to have someone else pick out a present this special.

He scanned the names of shops lining Main Street, hoping for inspiration. The bright sign for Happy Paws Pet Shop caught his eye, but that wouldn't help him much. His grandmother didn't own a single pet, nor did anyone in his family. They were all too busy with their various careers.

An older lady hurried out of the shop with a white, fluffy dog in her arms. She swooped down and set the dog on the sidewalk. "Come on, Princess." He smothered a smile when he saw the dog's collar perfectly matched the blue shade of the lady's heels, which, come to think of it, were a strange choice in shoes for a casual beach town.

The lady looked up and stared at him for a minute, but he quickly ducked his head and turned away. He glanced back over his shoulder and saw her hurrying down the sidewalk, the little dog scurrying at her side.

He looked at his reflection in the store window in

front of him. *He* could barely recognize himself, so he should be okay, right? He looked down the street, and another sign caught his eye—Coastal Creations. *That's right.* He remembered Shawna Jacobson raving about the shop when he'd mentioned he was headed to Indigo Bay. She'd bought some kind of necklace there and posted on social media about it. Evidently, the post had gone viral, and these necklaces were the hot thing after that. Not that his grandmother was trendy. She was traditional. But maybe the shop would have something.

With determined strides, he headed off to see if the shop could solve his dilemma.

Whitney Layton looked up from where she sat behind the counter, wrapping a piece of sea glass carefully in thin, silver wire. Sunshine spilled in through the open door. A man stood outside perusing her displays in the shop windows. He looked through the window and caught her staring at him and lifted a hand in a brief wave. She smiled at him, hoping he'd come on inside. She'd had few customers in the shop today, though the online orders had been coming in steadily, like the custom piece she was working on now.

The man entered the store, and she put down her work. "Welcome. May I help you?"

He crossed over to the display case she was sitting behind, slipped off his sunglasses, and hooked them on the neckline of the t-shirt he was wearing. "I hope so. I'm looking for something special. Something different. It's for my grandmother's eightieth birthday." He flashed a disarming grin. "Though, to be honest, we're not really sure how old she is. She's been stretching the truth for years, and we just go with it."

"Did you have anything particular in mind?"

"I'm... well, I'm hopeless at this. I have no idea. I just know she loves this town. She started coming here to Indigo Bay to vacation when she was younger... *much* younger. So we decided to throw her birthday party here. I thought a jewelry piece from the town might hold special meaning for her."

"I have some necklace and bracelet sets over here." Whitney slid from behind the counter and led the way to a display on the wall. "Or I could make a custom piece for you. When is her birthday?"

"About two weeks." His eyes held a bit of panic in the corners of their sky-blue depths.

"How about something like this?" She held up a silver necklace with a piece of emerald green sea glass embedded into a hammered silver drop. "I have the matching bracelet to it, also."

"I... I just don't know." The man frowned and walked along the wall. "How about something like this one? But do you have more green sea glass? Her favorite color is emerald green like that other set you showed me."

"I could make up one similar to this with green sea glass."

"Could it be ready in two weeks?"

"I do have a surcharge for a rush custom order, but I can squeeze it in. It's not every day a person turns eighty."

He smiled at her again with that utterly charming smile. "Or, whatever age she's actually turning."

"If you come over here, I'll write up the order. I require a deposit, then the balance is due when you pick it up."

"Sounds fair to me." He followed her over to the computer.

She entered the details of the order and an estimate of the cost. He didn't blink an eye at the price. "And your name?"

He paused, then nodded. "Richard Nicholson."

"Okay, Mr. Nicholson. Can you tell me where you're staying here in town and give me your cell phone number?"

"I'm not sure of the address. It's two houses on the bay. Two huge pink houses."

"Ah, The Pink Ladies. Both of them? They're beautiful homes. I'm sure you'll enjoy them."

"Yes, we rented both of them. The whole family is coming in. I came early to make sure everything is ready for the big event. They'll all be trailing in over the next week or so. Then the party is the weekend after next."

"Your phone number so I can call when it's ready?"

"I… uh… I'll just check back in with you."

Whitney frowned at his answer, but he was holding out his credit card, so she took it from him and ran it. It went through flawlessly, so she figured everything was okay, even if he didn't want to give her his number.

She handed him a receipt for his down payment. "Here you go. If you give me a week, I'll know better when I'll be finished. I promise to have it done before the party, though."

"Thanks, I appreciate that."

"Thanks for coming in. I hope your grandmother will be pleased with her gift."

"Me, too." Mr. Nicholson stepped back. "I'll be back in about a week."

"I'll see you then."

Whitney watched as he paused in the doorway, slipped on his sunglasses, and adjusted his cap down lower over his eyes. He disappeared out into the sunshine.

## CHAPTER 2

W hitney walked along the shoreline early the next morning. She loved catching the sun rising over the sea. This morning did not disappoint. She plopped down on the sand and watched while the sky lightened and the sun tossed colors of pink and orange into the clouds scattered over the horizon.

She turned away from the view at the sound of someone approaching.

"Morning." The man—*Richard Nicholson, wasn't it* —from the shop yesterday walked up to her. "I see I've found another sunrise watcher."

"I do love the sunrise. I try to make it out here to the beach every week or so to catch it."

"Mind if I join you?"

"Not at all. Pull up some sand." She grinned at him.

Mr. Nicholson sank to the sand beside her and

stretched out his long legs. His sunglasses were perched on his head, but no ball cap today. He had thick brown hair that blew in the breeze, and the faintest hint of whiskers covered his face.

"I didn't catch your name yesterday." His words interrupted her thoughts.

"It's Whitney. Whitney Layton."

"Nice to officially meet you, Miss Layton." He flashed that captivating smile again.

Where did someone learn to smile like that? It was the most charismatic smile she'd ever seen. "Um, it's just Whitney. Call me Whitney." She brought her thoughts from his dashing smile and looked out at the sunrise. The sun broke through the clouds sitting on the horizon, and rays of light danced on the waves.

"Nice view." Mr. Nicholson stared out at the sea.

"It is." She mindlessly picked up a handful of sand and let the grains filter through her fingers. "I never get tired of it."

"Do you live here in town?"

"I do. Lived here my whole life." She turned and smiled at him. "Where are you from?"

"I currently live in Los Angeles."

"You're a long way from home."

"Not sure I'd call L.A. home, but I've been there for a while."

"What do you do there?"

"I'm… I'm between jobs right now."

"Oh." She didn't know what to say to that. Was he

looking for work? Had he been without a job for long? He didn't seem like the drift-through-life type, but what did she know? She'd only just met him.

"You're so right about The Pink Ladies." His words interrupted her running thoughts on his job situation. "I looked through both of them yesterday. Very nice. I figured since I was the first to get here, and I'm doing most of the work planning the party, that I'd get my pick of the rooms."

"Bet I know which room you picked."

He eyed her. Which one?"

"Well, if I were staying there, I'd pick the turret room. I've seen the photos on the real estate website. Windows all around. So nice and what a view of the bay."

He laughed. "Yes, that's the one I picked. It is nice."

She glanced at her watch. "Well, I better go. I have lots of work to get done today."

"I hear you have a custom jewelry piece to get started on, too." He tossed her yet another entrancing smile.

She was going to have to find a way to break the spell of his smiles...

He stood up in one fluid motion. "Can I walk you back to your shop?" The pretty blonde woman

—*Whitney*—looked up at him. He held out a hand and she slipped her hand in his. He effortlessly eased her to her feet, and she dusted the sand from her shorts with her delicate hands.

"Sure. You headed that way?" She reached up and shoved some curls away from her face.

"Yep." He hadn't really planned on heading back to Main Street, but it seemed as good of an idea as any. His other choice was to go back to The Pink Lady and have a lonely bowl of cereal from the well-stocked pantry. His assistant had made sure both houses were stocked with essentials.

They headed into town, a short walk down Bayview Avenue, then crossed over to Main Street. He regretted he'd forgotten his ball cap this morning when he'd left the house, but he did have his sunglasses at least. Not many people were around this early on Main Street anyway. It was probably safe.

They walked up to the door of Coastal Creations. Whitney took a key from her pocket and opened the door. She turned to him. "It was nice seeing you again."

"You, too."

Just then another woman hurried up to them. "Hey, Whit, I was hoping I'd catch you this morning. Here, I brought you coffee."

The woman paused and stared at him. He shifted uneasily from foot to foot.

"I… sorry, I only brought two cups." The woman frowned while she stared at him.

"That's okay. I was just leaving." Leaving quickly. Before this woman figured it out. "I'll talk to you later, Whitney." He spun around and hurried off down the street.

Whitney took the welcomed cup of coffee from Meredith's outstretched hand—though most people in town called her Merry. "Thanks."

Her friend looked a bit… stunned.

"You, okay?"

"You didn't tell me he was in town." Merry looked at her accusingly.

"That *who* was in town?" She frowned. "You know Richard Nicholson?"

Merry bobbed her head, and her brown hair swept across her shoulders. "Don't you know who that is?"

"You're talking in circles. Please try and make some sense." She walked into the shop with Merry right behind her.

"Whit, that was Rick Nichols."

She frowned. "*Richard Nicholson.*"

"Rick Nichols. The actor."

"Do I know him?"

"You've got to get out more". Merry's brown eyes flashed with exasperation. "Of course you do. He starred in that movie, The Humbleton Castle, with Shawna Jacobson.".

Whitney searched her memory. She knew who

Shawna Jacobson was because the actress had single-handedly made her shop famous after her viral post about the jewelry she'd purchased at Coastal Creations. *But this Rick guy?*

"You remember the movie. We went to see it together in Charleston at The Movie Mecca. It was that romance about a rich guy and the poor girl set at a castle that was made into a B&B."

"I kind of remember that." She did. Sort of. She was pretty sure that was the last movie she'd gone to see, and it had been a couple of years ago.

"Seriously, what am I going to do with you?" Merry set her bag on a display and pulled out her phone. She tapped on the screen for a moment, then flashed the phone at Whitney. "See, this movie. Remember?"

She squinted at the picture. "*Now* I remember it. Romantic comedy set at that gorgeous castle."

"Well, I'm positive that guy was Rick Nichols."

"Richard Nicholson. Rick Nichols." She pursed her lips. "Too much of a coincidence, right?"

"Rick Nichols must be a stage name." Merry snatched back her phone and searched again. "Yep, it says here on the actor database that his real name is Richard Nicholson."

"Hm, well, I didn't recognize him." Well, that explained his captivating smile. They probably taught that in acting school. Did all actors go to acting school? She had no clue.

"I don't know what I'm going to do with you. I

try so hard to keep you current." Merry laughed. "You live in your own little world."

"Hey, I *like* my own little world." Whitney grinned and took a sip of her coffee. Her quiet, simple little world. She loved her life in Indigo Bay. Though she wouldn't mind letting him brighten her world for a few weeks with that smile of his. She had to admit he was rather easy to look at.

What was she thinking? She'd maybe see him one more time when he came to pick up the gift. This wasn't a movie and she wasn't some actress playing a part.

She shook her head. Anyway, she didn't need any more unwanted attention, she'd seen what chaos like that brought to her shop.

Rick stood in front of the desk at city hall, his feet firmly planted until he got a better answer, the answer he wanted to hear. "What do you mean I don't have the pavilion reserved for the weekend after next? I specifically reserved it online. I did it months ago. I have a confirmation number. The email I received said all I need to do was to come by city hall and pick up the permit. I've hired a band. Everything is *all set*."

"I'm sorry, I don't see you listed. It's already taken by the Ashland Belle Society."

Rick tapped on his phone and pulled up his

confirmation email. "Here, my confirmation number is three-four-eight-a-c."

The lady typed his confirmation number into her computer. "Oh, I see the problem."

"There is no problem. I reserved the pavilion." He glared at her.

"Yes, you did. But it appears you reserved it for *next* year."

"What?" He looked at the confirmation email on his phone. She was right. He'd messed up and reserved *next* year, not this year. How could he have made such a ridiculous mistake? Christina was going to kill him... His sister would *not* have a sense of humor about the mess-up.

"I don't suppose there's another place in town like that pavilion that I could rent out?"

"There are a few places around town, but they would all be rented at this late date." The lady's face held a look of triumph for being right.

When he was so very wrong. His heart pounded in his chest. He couldn't mess this up.

Now what was he going to do? He had a ton of family coming to town and friends of his grandmother invited to the party... and no place to have the darn thing. He shoved his phone back in his pocket.

He knew the look he'd see on his parents' faces when they heard the news of how he'd screwed this up. Just one more thing in a long list of ways he'd disappointed them. Like becoming an actor instead of a lawyer like his brother or a surgeon like his sister.

He ran his fingers through his hair. The hair that still wasn't covered with a ball cap, and he was pretty sure the woman he'd run into in front of Whitney's shop had figured out who he was.

Nothing was going according to plan.

# CHAPTER 3

W hitney closed the door to her shop and locked it behind her. She could almost hear her brother's voice in her head warning her to lock the door every single time she left. He didn't want any repeats of the break-in from last summer. She smiled to her herself. Will was way too overly protective anyway, but she'd almost gotten used to it. Almost.

She looked at her watch, trying to decide what to do for dinner. Choices. She could go home to eat, but she'd have to stop and pick up groceries if she did that. She was forever letting her food pantry go bare in the busy summer season when she worked long hours at the shop. There wasn't enough energy left in her body after the long day to both grocery shop and cook.

Sweet Caroline's sounded like a much better choice. She headed down the street to the restaurant.

"Hi, Whitney." Caroline greeted her with a warm smile as she entered the cafe.

"Hi. Just came in for a quick bite. You know, like I already have twice this week. I really am going to make grocery shopping a priority. Soon." She smiled at the owner.

"Well, you're welcome here anytime." Caroline led her to a table by the window. "I'll send the waitress over for your order."

She sank into the chair, grateful to be off her feet. It had been a busy day at the shop, and she hadn't had much time to sit down and work on the jewelry piece she was designing for that Richard-Rick guy.

As if conjured up from her thoughts, the door to the restaurant opened and Rick came through the doorway, a ball cap on his head and unneeded sunglasses resting on his face. She watched while he took off the glasses and looked around the cafe. He spied her, and she lifted a hand in a wave.

He crossed over to her table. "Hi, there. Looks like we keep running into each other today." He sent her that lethal weapon smile. The one that made her mind go blank.

"Uh, it does." Whitney looked up at him, searching for words. "Um… are you meeting someone here, or would you like to join me? I just sat down and haven't ordered yet." She was just being friendly, it wasn't that smile of his. Of course, now that she knew he was a movie star, she figured that smile was just part of his act. But what was she thinking, asking *a movie star* to join her?

"Not meeting anyone and I'd like to join you." He slipped into the chair across from her.

The waitress came, they both ordered, then silence hung over the table. Rick shifted in his seat. She fiddled with her napkin. She couldn't get past the fact she was sitting here at Sweet Caroline's with an actor —and a *famous* actor according to Merry.

"Did you get started on the jewelry piece?" He finally broke the silence.

"Barely. It was a busy day at the shop. But don't worry, I'll have it in time for the party."

He scowled. "If we even have a party."

"What do you mean?"

"I screwed up. I rented that big pavilion at your city park for the party… but I messed up and put in the wrong year when I reserved it. *Who does that?* Some Belle Society has it rented. Where am I ever going to find a big enough place to have the party at this late date?"

She frowned. "That's a pretty big mess-up."

"Yes, *thank you*, I know." He let out a long breath of air.

"No, I didn't mean it like that." She quickly apologized. "We can fix it though, I bet."

"We?"

"I mean, we could come up with a solution."

A hopeful expression settled on Rick's face. "Like what?"

"How about if you rented a tent for the party? There's that large flat area between the two Pink Ladies. You could just adapt things a bit. String lights on the tent. It could look kind of magical."

"I've already hired a band."

"You can get those dance floors that they put down. Part of the tent could have room for the band and the dance floor. Tables around the edge."

His eyes brightened. "That might work."

She loved how he perked up as she helped him solve his dilemma. Maybe he'd flash one of those smiles of his...

"You could possibly put the food and bar up on one of the decks. That would leave more room under the tent."

"I think this might work. All day I've been beating myself up, thinking we'd have to cancel the party, or at least downsize it to just our family and have it in one of the houses. But this sounds like the perfect solution."

"I know of a place in Charleston where you can rent all that. The tent, tables, and chairs. They might even have the dance floor." She pulled out her phone and scrolled through the contacts. She paused, knowing he'd shied away from giving her his phone number before. "I can write the information down."

"Ah, no. Just text it to me." He gave her his number.

Should she put it in her phone as Richard Nicholson or Rick Nichols? She rolled her eyes at her indecision. Like it mattered. She typed in Richard Nicholson—she'd go along with his charade—and sent him the information.

The waitress brought their meals, and they settled into a comfortable conversation about the town.

"Have you ever been here before?" Whitney took a sip of her drink.

"No. Always meant to since my grandmother speaks so highly of it. She comes here fairly regularly now that she's retired. She's asked me to come with her a few times, but I've always been too busy."

"That's nice she likes to visit often. We do like our regulars." She wondered if she knew his grandmother. She did get to know some of the long-time regular visitors to the town. "What's her name? I may know her."

Rick sat with a deer-in-the-headlights expression on his face. "Um…"

Rick paused, not sure he wanted to answer Whitney's question, but how could he not? He drew in a long breath. "My grandmother is Viola Lemmons."

He watched while the inevitable recognition spread across her face.

"The actress?"

"The very same one."

"Wow." She sat with a surprised look on her face. Then she frowned. "So, that explains it."

"Explains what?"

"Well, you're Rick Nichols, aren't you? Merry said you were. Richard Nicholson. Rick Nichols. It doesn't take much of a stretch…"

He had to admit, it stung a little that it took her friend to explain who he was. Whitney hadn't even recognized him. Which was what he wanted, right? A few days where no one knew his name. Only… if he could get a few more good roles, maybe he would be more recognized, more famous. Then maybe everyone would think he'd made a success of his life. Maybe.

Which, once again, was what he also wanted, right?

He raked his fingers through his hair and sighed. "So you know who I am. I was hoping to keep my identity a secret for a while longer. Hoping for some, I don't know, normal days? Days where no one knows who I am."

"*I'm* not going to tell anyone." She looked indignant.

But somehow it always came out who he was. Cameras would flash. Tabloids would write stories, true or not.

"So, you're following in your grandmother's footsteps?"

"Sort of. Though she has big footsteps to follow. She's very well-known. A talented actress, and I'm not just saying that because she's my grandmother." He was very proud of her. She'd not only hit it big when she was younger, she'd continued to do many big roles as she'd aged. Everyone recognized her name. She was famous. Unlike him. He was more… well-known, or even maybe it was just *known*. Kind of.

Whitney hadn't recognized him.

So there he was, back at it again. *What was it he really wanted?*

They walked out of Sweet Caroline's and into the warm night. The lights along Main Street illuminated the sidewalks. A couple walked by eating ice cream cones. Rick was suddenly, desperately craving a butter pecan ice cream cone.

"Well, thanks for joining me for dinner." Whitney turned to him.

"So, where do you think that couple got their ice cream?" He watched, longingly, as they walked away.

"At the ice cream shop right down the street, The Trixie Cone."

"I think I'm going to pop in there and get a cone for my walk home."

Whitney's eyes lit up. "Really? Ice cream sounds good to me, too."

"Well, lead the way."

They entered the shop. Red cafe tables were scattered around the room, and a large chalkboard behind the counter listed their multitude of flavors.

Whitney walked up to the counter and greeted

the woman working there. "Hey, Trixie. How's it going?"

He watched while Trixie stared at him for a moment, then ducked her head.

She'd recognized him. *Probably.*

*Maybe.*

*Or not.*

He was beginning to doubt anyone even knew who he was. Maybe he was just a legend in his own mind. He put his attention back on the chalkboard of flavors, though he knew he'd end up with butter pecan.

He ordered his ice cream and Whitney ordered chocolate fudge. They wandered outside and down the street, eating their desserts.

"So, I guess you know everyone in town?" He took a lick of the delicious dessert before it dripped all over him.

Whitney grinned at him. "Almost everyone."

"That must be so... *strange*?"

"Why do you say that?"

"Don't they always know your business and what you're doing?"

"Probably." She shrugged. "But I like knowing most of the people I see here. At least the townspeople. Even some of the repeat tourists. Lots of people come back here year after year."

A drip of ice cream ran down his chin, and he swiped at his mouth. "This is really good. I mean, really, *really* good."

"Best ice cream in Indigo Bay." Whitney stopped. "This is where I head this way, and you head that way back to The Pink Ladies."

"I… could walk you home. I mean, if that's okay with you." He was always asking to join her, wasn't he?

"You sure? You'll have to double back afterward to get to the bay side of town. I live on the ocean side."

"Yep, I'm sure."

They fell into step, walking and finishing up their ice cream. They ambled down Seaside Boulevard, and she led him up to the door of a cute, little, mint-green cottage.

"This is me."

He wondered if she was going to invite him in, but she climbed the steps to the porch without asking him.

"Well, thanks for walking me home."

"You bet. It's a nice night out."

"You know how to get back to The Pink Ladies?"

"Yep."

"Well, I'll see you." Whitney turned, unlocked the door, and slipped inside with a slight wave of her hand.

He slowly turned around, his footsteps crunching on the crushed shell drive. He turned back once and saw the inside of the cottage illuminated with light, like a cheerful, welcoming home. A big contrast to his modern, interior-designer-decorated apartment in L.A. Cheerful or welcoming were about the least likely words anyone would use to describe it. Not that he was there very much. He was often off on location, or if he worked in town, the hours were long and grueling. When he was in between jobs, he often left the city.

He scowled. He hadn't really thought about it before, but his apartment in Los Angeles really held no appeal to him at all. He realized he didn't ever think of it as home.

He turned away again and slowly strolled through the streets of Indigo Bay, across the town to the bay side. He walked up the stairs to Pink Lady One where he was staying. No lights welcomed him here, either. He unlocked the door and walked into the dark, silent house.

# CHAPTER 4

Finally, something was working out for the birthday gala for his grandmother. Whitney's connection in Charleston set him up with everything he needed. The tent, chairs, tables, and even the dance floor. Whitney had saved him from the wrath of his sister and the disappointed looks from his parents. He just needed to convince Christina that this change was on purpose and a better option for the party. No need for her to find out he'd booked the pavilion for the wrong year. No need at all...

He sat at a table at Pink Lady One with a pad of paper in front of him, crossing things off his list. He looked out at the bay while a large cruiser slid across the water and into the nearby marina. He'd gone on a long weekend cruise on a huge yacht after his last movie had wrapped up. It hadn't turned out exactly as the relaxing trip he'd planned. Shawna Jacobson had been on the cruise and someone had grabbed photos of them together and blasted them all over social media. His agent ran with it and did his best to promote them as a couple.

*Which they weren't.*

At times he thought Shawna might wish they were a couple, but he knew her well. She'd drop him in a heartbeat if a more famous actor came along.

He stood and wandered over to the window, watching a lone blue heron walk along the waterfront in awkward strides. He glanced at his phone to check the time.

Seemed like as good a time as any to take a break from his to-do list. Maybe he'd head over to Coastal Creations and see how Whitney was doing on the necklace. Yes, that was the reason he wanted to go see her. Just to check on the necklace.

And maybe, while he was there, he'd ask her out to dinner. Not as a date, really. But as a thank you for helping him and giving him a solution to his *Pavilion Problem* as he'd begun to think of it. He grabbed his hat and sunglasses from the table.

He went outside and climbed down the stairs of the long front porch. He glanced over at the red sports car but decided to walk instead. It wasn't far to Whitney's shop, and the day sprinkled warm sunshine all over the town.

He strolled down the streets, debating on whether to grab another ice cream cone at The Trixie Cone but decided against it. A couple of weeks of eating everything he wanted and not going to the gym wasn't going to help him any with landing the next role he was hoping to get. He looked wistfully through the window as he determinedly passed by the ice cream shop. As if to torment him a little bit more, a couple came out of the shop, laughing and licking on ice cream cones. He smiled a forced smile at them and walked on by.

He pushed through the door of Whitney's shop, and a friendly bell announced his entrance. She looked up from where she was sitting behind the counter, her head bent over her work, and smiled when she saw him.

"Come look. I've started on your grandmother's jewelry. I found some wonderful pieces of emerald green sea glass."

Her smile and eager words were impossible to resist. He crossed over to where she was working. She'd spread out a collection of sea glass and sorted out a few bright emerald pieces.

"Those are great. My grandmother has emerald green eyes and loves to wear that color. This is going to be perfect."

"Well, I hope you like it when I get it all made up."

"I'm sure I will." Whitney made very creative jewelry pieces, and this was one thing he was confident of in his gala planning. He was sure his grandmother would love this jewelry set. Who knew he had the ability to pick out the perfect gift?

"You just out for a walk today? It's a lovely day.

One of those perfect summer days we're known for. Not too hot, and a nice gentle breeze."

"It is a perfect day. And your rental suggestion in Charleston had everything I needed. I can't thank you enough for saving the gala."

"I wouldn't say I exactly *saved* it."

"Close enough." Not to mention she saved him from embarrassing himself in front of his family with a failure to pull off the party after assuring them he had it all under control. Not that any member of his family had actually believed he could do this.

"Well, I'm glad it worked out." She shoved a few wisps of blonde curls away from her face. He tried not to stare at her delicate hands with their pale pink nails. Or her hair. Or her eyes. Her blue eyes the color of the sky on this perfect summer day.

"I actually... well, I was wondering..." Since when did he turn into a stuttering fool? "I wondered if I could take you to dinner. Just to say thank you for your help." He hurried to add that caveat.

"Well, sure, I guess."

Not the overwhelming acceptance he'd been hoping for. "I know it's very last minute, but would you like to go tonight? I thought I'd make a reservation at a place in Charleston called Bistro Fifty."

"I've never been there. I'd love to go."

"The reviews I read sounded like it's really great. If I pick you up at seven, would that work?"

"It would. I actually have help coming in the shop tonight, so I can leave a bit early."

"Perfect. I'll see you at seven." He turned to walk away before she saw what he knew was a silly grin on his face. He was ridiculously happy that she'd said yes to his invitation.

~

Merry perched on the end of Whitney's bed. She tilted her head to one side. "Not that one. It's too casual."

"Well, how fancy is this place?" Whitney scowled. She liked the dress she'd tried on. A simple, casual sundress.

"Well, I looked Bistro Fifty up online and read some reviews."

"You did?" She stared at her friend.

"Of course I did. Right after you called me. I didn't want to steer you wrong." Merry popped off the bed. "I wonder what the fifty stands for in the name. Or maybe it's just a trendy thing to put a number in the restaurant name."

She marveled at her friend. She would never have thought to look up the place. "Okay, so what should I wear?"

"How about the blue dress you have? It brings out the color of your eyes."

She rooted through her closet to the very back and pulled out a simple royal blue linen dress. She held it up and eyed it. She rarely wore it because linen wrinkled so badly, but she did think it looked good on her. "Okay, I'll try this one on."

She slowly turned around in front of the full-length mirror after she'd slipped on the dress. "Okay, I think this was a good choice."

"Yes, it's perfect." Merry nodded. "Now, you need to wear heels with it."

"I was thinking about just wearing my black flats."

"Of course you were. Which is exactly why you have me as the perfect friend. Wear heels."

Whitney sighed and looked through the shoe boxes on the upper shelf of her closet. The shoe boxes that held shoes she rarely wore. She found the box with some cream-colored heels and slipped them on. "I hope I don't trip in these."

Merry grinned. "You'll be fine. Sometimes I think that being your friend is a full-time job."

"Very funny." She stuck her tongue out.

"Now, let's find you the perfect necklace."

"Ah, now jewelry, that I can do." Whitney opened the large top drawer of her dresser and picked out a simple but elegant necklace she'd made.

Merry jumped up to fasten the necklace. "That looks perfect. Your jewelry is always so lovely."

"Thank you."

"Now, I'm going to fix your hair."

"What do you mean fix it? It's basically a pixie cut with a few longer wisps."

"I brought some texturing gel to keep it under control."

"Some what?" She eyed her friend.

"Sit. I promise you'll like it." Merry opened a small container and rubbed some white pasty-looking goo on her hands. She slid her fingers through Whitney's hair, then picked at some locks until she was satisfied. "Go look in the mirror."

She got up, walked back over to the mirror, and looked at her reflection. She had to admit that her hair did look nice. Just a bit of texture to her short locks. The blue dress and heels also looked nice, she grudgingly admitted to herself. "Thanks, Merry. I'd never have pulled this off without you. I mean, what do I know about what one wears when they are going out with a movie star?"

"You look perfect." Merry squeezed Whitney's shoulders. "Now, do you have a purse other than that old beat up one?"

"Over in the dresser. Second drawer."

Merry crossed over and brought back a simple clutch bag. "Give me your purse. I'll put your wallet and cell phone in here. Oh, and some lipstick."

"You think of everything."

"Hey, I've been waiting a long time for you to go on a real date. I want you to get it right."

She wanted to get it right, too. Her pulse raced with just the thought of going out with someone famous. What did she know about going out with someone used to the jet-set crowd? But then, as soon as she thought of him as *just Rick*, it made her feel better.

They both turned at the sound of a knock at the door. Whitney took a deep breath.

"You going to answer that?" Merry grinned at her.

"Yes. I guess I'm ready."

"You are. You look perfect, trust me."

Rick stood at the door of Whitney's cottage, a small bouquet of flowers clutched in his hand. He'd no idea why he was so nervous. It wasn't like he didn't go out on dates quite a bit. There was always some function his agent wanted him to go to. But somehow, this woman had managed to do what the most famous actress, or heiress, or anyone he'd dated had never done. She'd set him on edge and made him as nervous as he'd been on his first audition.

The door swung open, and the woman he'd run into at Whitney's shop stood in the doorway. "Hi, I'm Merry. I was just leaving." She slipped past him. "Oh, nice touch on the flowers." The woman grinned. "You two have a good time."

Then Whitney stood in front of him, looking so different than the woman who owned Coastal Creations and her simple, casual everyday style. Not that he minded her everyday look, but she looked stunning tonight.

"You look great."

She gave him a tentative smile. "Thank you." She nervously ran her hand along the side of her dress.

"Oh, these are for you." He stepped inside and handed her the flowers.

"Thank you. I'll go put them in a vase." She disappeared, then came back with the flowers in a vase and set them on a table. "They're very pretty."

He cleared his throat. "You ready to go?"

"I am."

They walked outside and he held the door open for her to get into the red sports car. She slid into the passenger seat, offering him a good look at her long, tanned leg. He carefully closed the door behind her and walked around the car, getting his bearings. This woman had a way of knocking his senses off kilter.

He got into the car and the engine started with a low, purring growl. "Okay, off we go."

They headed into Charleston, and Whitney sat quietly clutching her handbag. He knew he should start up a conversation, but words were failing him.

*Say something.*

"So, do you go into Charleston often for dinner?" *That was the best he could come up with?*

"Not often. Honestly, I'm usually so busy at the shop that I rarely even leave Indigo Bay. My brother keeps bugging me to come see him on Belle Island on the gulf coast of Florida, but I haven't made time to do that in ages."

"Any other family?"

"My father. He recently moved back to Indigo Bay after being gone for years."

"That must be nice for you."

"It's an… adjustment. We were estranged for years, but I think we've worked things out." She pressed her hand against her dress. "How about you? Family?"

"Ah, yes. I have family. My grandmother, of course. A brother and sister, my parents, nieces, aunts and uncles, and I've lost count of how many cousins."

"Wow, that's a lot. It's just my father, my brother, and I. I can't imagine having a big family like that."

He hadn't really thought about it. He did come from a huge family. He'd just accepted that was his life. Even if they were critical of him. Even if they drove him nuts at times. He guessed he was lucky to have that much family. *Usually.* "Well, most of them will be here for the gala. My brother will be here, and my sister will be here with her kids and stay at one of The Pink Ladies. So will my grandmother and my parents. A couple of aunts will be here with their broods. They all are staying around Indigo Bay or in Charleston. A lot of my grandmother's friends are coming, too."

"Sounds like it will be huge."

"A couple hundred people, I guess."

"Wow."

He didn't think it was *that* many people. He was used to huge shindigs in L.A. A couple hundred people were barely called a party in his circles. "Well, my grandmother does have a lot of friends, plus our family. It's a lot, I guess."

He pulled up in front of Bistro Fifty, and a valet opened the door for Whitney as he slid out of the driver's seat. He tossed the keys to the valet and took Whitney's arm. A young woman walked up to them and he paused.

"Oh, you're Rick Nichols, aren't you?"

He forced a smile and nodded. "I am."

"Could I get a photo with you? Please?"

"Of course." He knew that having his photo taken with fans was just part of his job, though Whitney looked a bit shocked.

The woman jumped beside them and snapped off a few selfies on her cell phone. "Thank you. *Thank you*. My friends will never believe I saw you—Rick Nichols—right here in Charleston."

"You're welcome."

The girl walked away, busily tapping into her phone as she walked. He took Whitney's elbow and led her into the restaurant. He noticed the stunned looked still plastered on her face.

"Mr. Nichols. We're so glad to have you here." The maitre d' hurried up to them. "I have reserved our best table for you."

"Thank you." Rick had to admit that having actor status sometimes helped with getting the perfect reservation at the perfect table. At least the restaurant had recognized him even if Whitney hadn't. He was going to get over that fact really soon. Maybe.

The man led them to their table and handed Rick an extensive wine list. "The wine steward will be over to take your order."

He nodded as he opened the wine list.

"Does that happen often?" Whitney's voice was barely above a whisper.

"Does what happen?"

"People stopping you to get their picture taken with you."

"Often enough. Hence the sunglasses and ball cap in Indigo Bay. Sometimes it's just easier to be incognito. But the fans are what make my job. More fans, better roles."

"It seems so... invasive."

It was a bother sometimes, he'd admit that, but he'd come to realize it was part of his life. "Guess it just comes with the territory."

"I don't think I could handle that." She shook her head. "I had a hard enough time when Shawna Jacobson bought jewelry from my shop and posted all over social media. I had reporters coming to do articles on me and my shop. It was so surreal. Though her doing that kind of made my shop the success it is now. It exploded with online sales as well as sales in the actual shop. I get a lot of custom orders."

"Like my grandmother's."

"Exactly."

"Well, the media attention might have attracted some business for you, but it's your talent that really sells the pieces."

She blushed a rosy pink. "Thank you."

"No, I mean it. Your jewelry pieces are stunning and very unique. I can't wait to give my grandmother the set you're making."

"I hope she'll like it."

"I'm sure she will." He glanced at the wine list again. "So, shall I order us some wine?"

"Yes, please. I usually prefer a drier white."

"Perfect, they have some unoaked white burgundy from the Alsace region."

"That's all French to me." She grinned. "But I'll trust you."

He ordered their wine and glanced around the room. Some of the patrons were looking at him surreptitiously, but thank goodness no one had actually gotten up and come over to their table. He wasn't sure Whitney would deal well with another intrusion.

## CHAPTER 5

Whitney tried not to let her eyes widen at the prices on the menu. Nor did she know what half the items on the menu were. Or the sauces. How would she know if she was ordering something she'd enjoy? She sighed, knowing she was going to have to admit her ignorance to Rick. Rick, the movie star who was used to dining in places like fancy French restaurants with fancy French words.

She looked across the table at him, his head bent over the menu. "Um, Rick?"

He looked up and smiled at her and she almost dropped her menu. When would she develop a force field that protected her from that smile? "I don't know what most of this stuff is." She smiled ruefully. "Or what *any* of it says."

"You're in luck. My grandmother speaks fluent French and taught me. Do you like chicken or fish? Maybe beef?"

He ordered her meal without making her feel foolish about her lack of knowledge, and they sat back and sipped on the wine he'd ordered. It was really good wine even if she knew nothing about unoaked wine and wasn't burgundy wine supposed to be red? She refused to ask him, unwilling to show any more of her cluelessness. Instead, she'd just fill the evening with small talk. That was safe. That was something she knew about.

"So, you said you have a brother and a sister. Where do they live?" She wanted to know more about Rick the person. Well, she wouldn't mind knowing more about Rick the actor, too, but she didn't want to sound like a groupie or something. Or were groupies just for rock stars? She wanted to know all the things about him, which bothered her a bit. She hadn't been this interested in a man in a long time. A very long time.

*So she decided to be interested in an actor who lived all the way across the country?* Not a very smart choice on her part.

Rick, oblivious to her rambling thoughts, answered her question. "My sister, Christina, lives in Philadelphia. That's where we grew up. She's a surgeon. My brother lives in D.C. He's a lawyer there. My parents have a place in both Philadelphia and D.C." He paused and took a sip of his wine. "My mother's a senator."

She sat back in silence. Actors, a doctor, a lawyer, and a senator for Pete's sake. You couldn't get a more degreed and notable family. She couldn't be any different from him if she tried. Far apart in distance *and* in upbringing.

"I'm just a mere actor. The family's black sheep." His eyes twinkled, but she could see the tiniest bit of hurt in their blue depths.

"So being a famous actor is a black sheep?"

"Well, I'm not *that* famous." He grinned. "You didn't know who I was when you met me."

She felt the heat of blush flush her face. "I'm sorry about that. I don't... I mean..." How to get out of this gracefully? "I don't see movies often, and I'm not a television fan. Merry says I live in my own little world... and it drives her nuts."

"No, I'm just teasing about you not recognizing me. As far as my family is concerned, I'm a very mediocre one, especially compared to my grandmother. My mother hoped I'd follow along in her footsteps in politics, or at least go on to law school. But, to her great chagrin, I never finished college and moved out to Los Angeles."

"But your grandmother must be pleased."

"I think she is. I doubt if I'll ever reach her level of famousness—is that even a real word?"

She couldn't believe his family wouldn't be proud of him, but then she knew better than most that families could be difficult.

"You said your brother lives on an island in Florida?"

"Yes, he owns a tavern there on Belle Island." She

owned a jewelry business, Willy owned a tavern, and her father was a barely sober recovering alcoholic. She and her family were not even in Rick's league. But he'd only asked her out to thank her for her help. It wasn't like it was a real date or anything.

"So, you're both entrepreneurs." Rick stretched out his legs, and they bumped hers under the table. "Oops, sorry." He swung his legs to the side.

She liked the way he called them entrepreneurs. It sounded more... fancy. But since when had she not been proud of all that Will and she'd accomplished? They might not be actors, or doctors, or politicians, but they had both come a very long way from their upbringing.

The waiter delivered their meal, interrupting her torturously meandering thoughts. They ate their meal while their conversation turned to Indigo Bay. That was a safe topic for her, too.

They finished off their meal by splitting the most delicious chocolate something-or-other-French-named dessert that she'd ever tasted.

The maitre d' came over when they'd finished and leaned over to speak quietly to Rick. He answered, and the man hurried away. Rick frowned and took out his cell phone. With a few taps, his frown grew deeper. "Ah, I'm sorry, Whitney. Looks like we've been discovered."

He held out his phone, and she took it, looking at the photo. It was a photo of them with the young woman who had stopped them in front of the restaurant. Complete with the hashtags #RickNichols #newloveinterest                         #whoisshe #whereisShawnaJacobson?

Her heart plummeted at seeing the Shawna Jacobson hashtag. Was Rick *dating* Shawna? So why had he asked her, a simple shop owner, out?

To *thank her*, not for a real date.

She looked at the photo again. She was on Rick's arm with a startled expression on her face. Not a very flattering photo, not that it really mattered.

"The maitre d' said there are photographers waiting outside. They didn't let them in, of course. But it looks like we'll have to make a run through them when we leave."

"How did this happen?" She stared at the photo. "And so quickly?"

"It's the hashtags. Some photographers skim social media, looking for hashtags, hoping for a chance to catch photos of celebrities. I'm sorry you got dragged into this." He stood up.

"Let's go. They're bringing my car around. We might as well get this part over with."

She sat in her chair, unable to move, unable to process her thoughts.

"Whitney?" He held out a hand.

She slowly got to her feet. She let him tuck her hand on his elbow and lead her to the front door. As soon as the doorman opened the door, flashes went off, blinding her as she clung to his arm and he opened the car door for her. She slipped inside, dazed by the number of people outside and the constant bursts of lights.

Rick slid into the driver's seat and pulled away from the curb, the flashes of light still popping behind them as they sped away.

～

Rick glanced over at Whitney, sitting rigidly in the passenger seat of the car. She stared out her side window and said nothing to him. He drove on and let her sit with her thoughts, wishing she'd talk to him but knowing this date hadn't turned out quite like he'd hoped. Not that it was a date. It was a simple thank you. He'd gotten a little too comfortable with rarely being recognized in Indigo Bay that he hadn't expected the media attention in Charleston.

Finally, the silence got to him. "You okay?"

She turned to look at him. "I was just… surprised. I had no idea your life was like that. Photographers and fans, always snapping your photos."

"I'm sorry to put you through that. I should have been smarter about it. Gone somewhere less well-known. At least worn my sunglasses and cap."

"Yes, sunglasses at night would have been so subtle." She gave him a small smile. "Is it always like that for you?"

"Quite often."

"I couldn't stand the lack of privacy. People knowing my business and taking photos all the time."

"I guess you just get used to it in my field." He sighed. "But I admit it would be nice to escape it sometimes."

"I bet." She turned and looked out the window again.

When he got to Indigo Bay, he pulled into the drive in front of her cottage. A warm, welcoming light spilled through the front door and gently illuminated the porch. He climbed out of the car and came around to open the door for her. She slid out and started walking to her door but lost her balance on the crushed shells. He reached and quickly caught her as she fell against him. He wrapped his arm protectively around her, liking the feeling of her next to him.

"You okay?" He looked at her.

She laughed. "Yes, I'm just not used to walking in heels. Much less walking in them on a surface like crushed shells. Now you know my little secret."

He led her up the steps, carefully keeping hold of her arm so she wouldn't trip again, *not* just because he didn't want to lose his contact with her. As soon as she got to the porch, she reached down and slipped off her shoes.

"My other secret? These things have been killing my feet all evening. I'm much more a flip-flop girl."

He grinned at her. "Nothing wrong with flip-flops."

She opened the door and turned toward him. He could see a flash of indecision in her eyes. She looked down at her bare feet, wiggled her toes, then looked back up at him. "Um, do you want to come inside for a few minutes?"

"I'd like that." He followed her into the cottage, pleased she'd decided to ask him in.

She dropped her shoes in the corner and led the way to her kitchen. "I can fix you a drink. Beer? Wine? Soda?"

"A beer sounds great, but I better stick with soda. I kind of have this strict rule about drinking and driving. One drink only."

"If you don't mind leaving your car until tomorrow, you could walk back to The Pink Ladies."

He paused, eyeing the open fridge. "That sounds like a deal. I'll have a beer."

She reached in, grabbed a bottle, and handed it to him. "Here, you wrestle the cap off. I'm going to get a glass of wine for myself."

They took their drinks out onto her deck overlooking the ocean. The moonlit sky tossed silvery beams of light on the gently rolling waves. She sat down on an Adirondack chair and he took the one beside her.

"I love sitting out here in the evenings. I swear this deck is the best part of the cottage."

"It is nice and peaceful." Especially after the chaos of leaving the restaurant.

"I love having coffee out here in the mornings, too. Watching the sun rise up out of the horizon and throw colors across the sky. You should see the photos on my cell phone. I'm forever taking sunrise photos. There is something magical about that time of day."

He watched as she relaxed in her chair and sipped her wine. She pushed a wisp of hair away from her face and turned to catch him staring at her. She smiled. "What are you looking at?"

"Just… you. Glad to see you relax after all that mess at Bistro Fifty."

"I was just startled. I guess I didn't handle it well, I'm sorry. I know I was quiet on the car ride home. My mind was racing with thoughts and… I know none of it was your fault." She looked into his eyes. "I did have a good time with you though. The food was wonderful. Especially that chocolate dessert."

"I'm glad you enjoyed it." At least that part of the evening had turned out well. And this part was turning out pretty nicely, too.

"So, what's next on your to-do list for the big gala?" She settled back in her chair.

"I'm talking with the caterer to finalize all that. Reconfirming the band. It's a small four-piece group. They play a mix of oldies and some new music. They know a lot of classics from my grandmother's era. I think they'll be perfect."

"That does sound nice."

"I want to make sure everything is settled before my family starts coming to town this weekend. Christina and my two nieces will arrive on Saturday. My grandmother on Monday. My brother and the rest of the family comes in after that." He was going to make darn sure that everything was in place before his sister got here, so there would be no way she could second-guess his every decision. Or maybe she still would, but the decisions will have already been made.

"How old are your nieces?"

"Six. They're twins and I adore them. They have me wrapped around their little fingers." Ah, his adorable nieces. They were full of boundless energy and endless questions. He enjoyed seeing them when he could get away, though that did mean he had to put up with his sister. He wished he and his siblings could get along better, but he was almost certain that unless he gave up acting and became something like a rocket scientist, they'd never think he'd amounted to anything. He tried hard not to let that bother him. It *didn't* bother him.

Mostly.

"I can't imagine a large family like yours. What's it like?"

"Well, it's noisy." He grinned. "Especially when all the kids come. My grandmother tries to get us all together at least once a year. Aunts, uncles, cousins. Usually a holiday party sometime in December. I don't catch it very often anymore."

"I always dreamed of growing up in a family like that. Lots of brothers and sisters and cousins. You're very lucky."

He couldn't miss the wistful look in her eyes. He'd never really thought much about coming from such a large family. It was just a part of him. He wondered what it would be like to only have a brother and a father for family. Maybe her family didn't even interfere in her life with millions of conflicting opinions of what she was doing wrong with her life…

"I guess I *am* lucky to have such a big family." Though, sometimes it sure didn't feel like it. Whitney made him feel like he should appreciate it more. She had a way of looking at the bright side of things, a habit he wished she'd teach him.

Right then he made up his mind to change his thinking. Instead of dreading his family coming to town, he was going to look forward to it. It was going to be a fabulous week of family togetherness. *How was that for positive thinking?*

## CHAPTER 6

Whitney rolled over and glanced at the clock. *Who in the world was calling her this early?* She snatched her cell phone from the bed table.

"Hey, sis."

"Willie, why are you calling me this early? Is everything all right?"

"You tell me."

She pulled the covers up and closed her eyes as she talked. "Um… you're the one who called me, remember?"

"I saw your photo in the news."

"What photo?"

"You and the actor. You know, what's-his-name, Rick Nichols."

She sat up straight in bed, the covers slipping down to her waist. "What? Where did you see that?"

"Pretty much everywhere. There was a big article about who is this mystery woman with Rick."

"Did any of the posts have my name?" She frowned.

"Not so far. So you're dating this actor guy and you didn't bother to tell your own brother?"

"No, I'm not *dating* him. He took me out to dinner as a thank you for helping him with a party he's planning for his grandmother."

"Hey, you realize his grandmother is Viola Lemmons, right?"

"Since when do you keep up with celebrities?"

"Ashley told me."

So her brother's girlfriend had seen it, too. Whitney scrubbed a hand over her face, trying to clear her foggy, just-woke-up mind. "I'm sure it will blow over soon. No one will figure out it was me. I'm a nobody."

"Whit, I'm pretty sure they'll dig around and find out who you are."

"Maybe not?"

"Maybe so. Look on the bright side, it might be good publicity for Coastal Creations."

She let out a long sigh. "This isn't what I planned. I do love that the shop is doing so well, but I don't like being in the spotlight. Not when Shawna Jacobson did that viral post. Not now."

"Well, I think you should be prepared. I'm pretty sure you're going to be in the limelight again."

"Well, Rick can just tell them he's not dating me." There, that was simple enough. Rick could deal with it. She climbed out of bed and headed to the kitchen in search of coffee. If she was going to be up this early, at least she could sip on coffee. The automatic coffee maker had done its thing. She reached for a mug and poured a steaming cup.

"Well, he can tell them you're not dating, but they might not listen."

"I'm sure it will all blow over soon. He's probably dating someone important or famous in Hollywood."

"There are rumors about him and Shawna Jacobson."

She took a sip of coffee. "And since when do you keep up with celebrity gossip?"

"You think I didn't check the guy out as soon as Ashley showed me the photo this morning?"

She smiled in spite of herself. Her big brother was always going to be overprotective. "Willie, don't worry about me. I'm sure it will all be over. Maybe no one will even figure out who I am."

"Hold on to that dream, sis. Gotta run. Call me if you need me."

She set the phone down on the counter and walked out onto the deck. A gentle sea breeze drifted in from the ocean. She turned her face to the sun, bathing in its warmth. Maybe this whole thing would just be a non-starter. It wasn't like it had been an actual date. Movie stars didn't *date* people like her.

Merry pushed through the door of Coastal Creations

minutes after Whitney opened the shop. "Whit, did you see all the photos of you online?"

Whitney sighed and sat on a stool behind the counter. "I did. Willie so kindly woke me up at the crack of dawn to inform me."

"Good thing I brought coffee." Merry handed her a cup.

Whitney figured she could use another cup after the morning she'd had. "Thanks."

"So, I was reading online, and they're all trying to figure out who you are. Won't be long before someone tells them."

"Maybe not?" She kept holding on to that hope, slim that it might be.

Merry tilted her head and scrunched up her face. "I could barely keep you sane when you got all that publicity from Shawna Jacobson about your shop, even though it turned out to be a very good thing for you. This might help the shop again, you know?"

"I'm not going to use my *friendship* with Rick to help the shop."

The bell over the door rang and Lucille Sanderson popped into the shop carrying her dog, Princess, in her arms. "Whitney Layton, you went out with a movie star," she said in a tone of total disbelief.

Which annoyed Whitney. "I went to dinner with Rick Nichols, yes." Did everyone in town see the photos?

"Well, that's just… amazing."

"Why is it so amazing? Whit is a talented, beautiful woman." Merry sprang to her defense.

"Oh, of course, she is, dear. It's not often that one of our own dates someone famous." Lucille petted Princess as she spoke, her perfectly manicured fingers threading through the dog's fur.

"It wasn't a *date*." Whitney wondered how many times she'd have to repeat that statement and to how many people.

"You went out to dinner with him. That's a date in my book." Lucille nodded emphatically. "Did you have a good time? The article I saw said you went to that new trendy restaurant, Bistro Fifty."

"The restaurant was nice." She did *not* want to discuss her non-date with Lucille—or with anyone. "But it was a one-time thing."

"If you say so, dear. But if it wasn't a serious date, maybe we could fix him up with my grandniece, Maggie?" Lucille looked hopeful.

"I think he's going to be busy with family stuff. He's in town throwing a birthday gala for his grandmother." Now, why had she given her any more information than absolutely necessary? She knew better than that. The whole town would know Rick's business by this afternoon, if not before.

"Well, you might mention her to him. She is such a lovely girl." Lucille turned to leave but glanced back over her shoulder. "Though, I still think your night out with him might be considered a date."

She rolled her eyes as Lucille slipped out of the shop.

Merry grinned at her. "Lucille will be stopping to talk to everyone she sees today to make sure they know about those online photos of you."

"Don't I know it. And I was hoping it would all just blow over."

"Don't count on it, Whit."

Rick slowly scrolled through his social media accounts on his computer. Photos of him and Whitney were plastered everywhere on various social media and news sites. He ran his fingers through his hair, then shut the laptop with a resounding click. He'd forgotten how things like this could get so out of hand. The media had him paired up and serious with Whitney after just one night.

As if she'd even want to speak to him again, much less be seen with him. He couldn't blame her. The media attention was his cross to bear, not hers. So far, he'd read no inkling that anyone had found out her name or anything about her. That much was good.

His phone rang. He glanced at it and saw a photo of his grandmother flash on the screen. He snatched the cell phone off the table. "Grandmere, how are you?"

"I'm fine, Richard. Are you enjoying your time in Indigo Bay?"

"I am. You're right, it's a charming little town. Things are coming along great for your big birthday party."

"I told you not to make a fuss about it."

Empty words. Rick knew darn well that his grandmother loved to have people fuss over her. "We want to do this for you."

"Well, you're sweet to go early and get things all set up. I have no doubt everything will be perfect. Besides, I know you needed a bit of a vacation. Now, do you like The Pink Ladies?"

"They are... *pink*. And huge. I'm staying in Pink Lady One."

"Did you get the turret room? It's so nice. I don't pick that room anymore to stay in, though I love it. I don't like climbing all those stairs anymore."

"I did choose that room. I have the big master suite on the main floor all set up for you."

"Thank you, dear. Oh, and did I hear something about you have a new young woman in your life? My assistant said she saw photos of you with someone new."

"She's just a friend. She helped me out with some... *details*... for the gala." He wasn't about to admit to his grandmother anything about the *Pavilion Problem*.

"Oh, is she from Indigo Bay? You should invite her to my party."

"I don't know if she'd want to come. She wouldn't really know anyone."

"She'd know you. If she's a friend of yours, I'd love to meet her. You should invite her over for drinks next week after I get to town. Promise me you'll do that."

He'd never been able to say no to his grandmother. "Okay, I'll see if she'll stop by."

"Perfect. I'll see you in a few days."

"Bye." He set his phone back on the table. It seemed like the whole world knew about his date with Whitney last night. The date that wasn't even a date. It was a *thank you*.

## CHAPTER 7

To heck with being concerned about what he was eating this week. It was going to be stressful enough without adding anything else to worry about. He grabbed his cell phone and headed outside. He was going to reward himself with another one of those fabulous ice cream cones from The Trixie Cone. He wasn't exactly sure what he was rewarding himself for. He hadn't gotten through much of his to-do list. He'd mainly browsed the internet looking for all the places photos from last night had turned up and feeling guilty for putting Whitney in the limelight.

His phone rang, and he pulled it out of his pocket.

Shawna.

He couldn't face talking to her right now. She'd evidently seen the photos, too. He slid the phone back in his pocket, feeling only *slightly* guilty for ignoring her call.

He entered the Trixie Cone and the woman behind the counter smiled at him. "Ah, Whitney's friend. You're back."

"I am."

The woman stared at him for a moment. "I usually remember faces. You look familiar. I mean besides being in here with Whitney."

Ah, his curse and blessing. Not quite famous enough for everyone to recognize him, but famous enough when some people did. "I probably just have one of those faces," he answered noncommittally.

"What can I get you today?"

"I'll have a butter pecan cone. Two scoops."

Just then the door to the shop opened and Whitney entered. She stopped when she saw him standing there, then a small smile—very small—crossed her face. "Hello, Rick."

"Rick. That's it." Trixie snapped her fingers. "Rick Nichols, right?"

Whitney walked up beside him. "Yes, he's Rick Nichols, but he's trying to keep it quiet around town, okay?"

"Sure thing." Trixie handed him his cone. "What can I get for you, Whitney?"

"Double chocolate fudge."

"You want to sit at one of the tables?" He wasn't sure if she'd agree to it, but took the chance.

"I… I guess so." She didn't look very certain of her answer.

They took their ice cream to the far corner table and sat down. He looked at her as she concentrated diligently on her cone, basically ignoring he was sitting right across from her. "So, I take it you found out our photos are everywhere."

She looked up at him and sighed. "I did."

"Sorry about that."

"It's not your fault."

"Well, of course it is. I'm the reason it happened."

She gave him that tiny smile again. "Okay, so it *is* all your fault."

He laughed. "Blame accepted."

"I've had a constant stream of people coming into the shop today to ask about it. I thought I'd escape to Trixie's and indulge in chocolate."

"Is it working?"

"It's starting to." Her blue eyes twinkled.

Whitney relaxed a bit and enjoyed her ice cream. She didn't know why she was letting those silly photos get to her.

The door to Trixie's opened again and Vicki Holloway and her daughter, Mia, walked in. Vicki looked over at Whitney and her eyes widened in unmistakable amazement. Whether it was more in seeing Rick or seeing *her* with Rick, she wasn't sure.

She ducked her head and concentrated on the cone, hoping Victoria would just leave them alone.

No such luck.

Vicki and Mia walked up to their table. "Well, Whitney. This is a surprise. Are you going to introduce me to your friend?" Vicki flipped her hair behind her shoulder and showered Rick with a glorious smile.

"Vicki, Mia, this is Rick. Rick, this is Vicki Holloway—I mean, Tanner—and her daughter, Mia."

"Whitney, you know no one calls me Vicki anymore. It's *Victoria*."

"Sorry, hard habit to break." She turned to Rick. "I've known Victoria since we were kids."

Rick smiled at Vicki-Victoria. "Nice to meet you." He then turned to Mia. "So, Mia. What flavor of ice cream is your favorite?"

She gave him a bashful smile. "I like Miss Trixie's homemade vanilla."

Victoria let out a long, exaggerated sigh. "I've tried everything to get this girl to experiment a bit, but she insists on vanilla every single time."

Rick winked at the girl. "You know what? I get butter pecan every single time. It's my favorite, so I figure why change?"

Mia grinned at his kind support of her only-one-choice-ever of ice cream.

Vicki ignored Rick's comment and the fact he gave her no sympathy for her long-suffering over having a child that only liked one flavor of ice cream.

"So, I saw you two were out at that new restaurant in Charleston. We really do have to go over and try it out soon. There just aren't many good places to eat here in Indigo Bay." Every word of Vicki's came out as haughty indictment of the town. She faced Rick while she spoke, ignoring Whitney completely.

"It was nice. But to be honest, I love Sweet Caroline's here in town."

Whitney wanted to jump up and hug him for coming to the town's defense. She didn't know why she let Vicki get to her.

"Well, if you want simple food, I guess so." Though Vicki shook her head no as she said it. "Anyway, I heard you're having a party for your grandmother's birthday. Too bad it's the same day as the Ashland Belle Society's auction at the pavilion here in town. Maybe you'll have time to stop by, though?"

"I'll be pretty busy the day of the party."

"That's a shame. Maybe you'd have something to donate? We're raising funds for the school."

"I'll see what I can do."

"You know, while you're in town, I'd love to have you over for dinner. My cook can do the most exquisite Southern cuisine. Not simple, it's more Southern with a twist." Vicki flashed her patented charming belle smile at Rick. "I'd love to show you some real Southern hospitality."

She wondered if Vicki could say Southern any more times in a row.

"Well, thank you for the invite, but I'm afraid I'm going to be very busy. My family is coming to town and I have the party to finish getting set up."

Vicki frowned. "Well, that *is* a shame."

She was insanely happy Rick had turned down Vicki's offer.

"Can we get our ice cream now?" Mia tugged at her mother's hand.

"Mia, how many times have I told you not to interrupt the grownups when they are talking?"

"Sorry." Mia looked down at her feet.

"Well, Whitney and I were just leaving, so I bet it's time for you to get your ice cream." Rick smiled at the girl and she looked at him shyly. "It was nice meeting you, Mia. And you, too, Vicki."

"Victoria," Vicki corrected. She took Mia's hand and led her away.

"You called her Vicki on purpose." Whitney smothered a grin.

He winked. "Yes, yes I did."

They escaped into the afternoon sunshine and left Vicki and Mia inside The Trixie Cone.

"You certainly have some... *interesting*... people here in Indigo Bay." Rick laughed, aware that Vicki had been flirting with him right in front of Whitney, not that Vicki had seemed to care what Whitney thought about that.

"Vicki has always been her own biggest fan. She decided, sometime after high school, that Victoria was a fancier name. She'll always be Vicki to me, though."

"To me, too." He laughed again.

"You were very nice to Mia."

"She's a cute kid."

"Poor Mia. She seems to never do anything quite right in her mother's eyes."

Rick could relate to that. He felt a sudden kinship to the young girl, trying to please her mother, never knowing when she was going to misstep.

"I should head back to the shop," Whitney interrupted his thoughts.

"Before you go, I was wondering…" He cocked his head and gathered his courage. "I was wondering if you'd like to go have dinner with me tonight."

She stood in front of him, a stunned expression plastered on her face. "You're kidding, right?"

"I was thinking something a bit less… photographic." He grinned at her. "Like maybe I could fix you dinner at The Pink Lady. I'm pretty handy with a grill."

"You want to cook for me?" Her tone bordered on incredulous.

"Don't sound so surprised. I have other talents besides acting." He looked at her, hoping for some sign that she'd say yes to his invite. "So, how about you say yes? I promise there won't be all the media attention we had last night. Just a nice, quiet meal."

"You don't have to do that. You've already done the thank you dinner thing." Whitney frowned.

"I think that dinner was more than you bargained for. Let me do this for you." He scrambled to come up with more reasons to convince her. "Besides, I don't really feel like eating alone. You'll be doing me a favor. How about it?"

He could see the exact moment he'd convinced her in the depths of her blue eyes. The blue eyes that mesmerized him and made him want to see them light up with her smile.

An unsure expression still covered her face. "Okay… What time should I come over?"

"I could pick you up," he offered.

"No, I'll just walk over."

"How about seven?"

"Okay, I'll see you then." Whitney turned and walked down the street toward Coastal Creations.

He grinned to himself and headed off to the market to buy groceries for dinner, whistling a tune under his breath.

## CHAPTER 8

"Seriously, Merry. Why did he ask me out again?" Whitney tapped her phone to change it to speaker mode so she could talk to her friend and still get ready.

"Because he likes you?" Merry's voice was filled with laughter. "You're panicking about what to wear again, aren't you?"

"No, I'm not," she lied as she stood in front of her closet at a loss.

"Wear that cute sundress you got a while ago. That teal one. It has some kind of floral print to it," Merry commanded her.

She reached into the closet and pulled out the sundress. "This might work."

"I gotta run, but Whit?"

"What?"

"No flip-flops." Merry's laugh came through the airways before the phone went silent.

She set the dress on the bed and dug around on the floor of her closet. She found a pair of simple white flats to wear. She got dressed, put on a bit of makeup, and surveyed herself in the mirror. Not bad. Not glamorous like a movie star, but okay for a small-town shop owner.

She glanced at her watch, then hurried to finish getting ready. She slipped out the door to the cottage with just enough time to walk over to the bay side of town. The closer she got to The Pink Ladies, the more nervous she got. *Why had she said yes?*

Before long she stood in front of Pink Lady One. The wide steps beckoned her, but she stood at the bottom of them, ignoring their call and gathering her courage. She looked both directions to see if anyone would notice her entering the house, especially anyone with a camera. Satisfied with the lack of prying eyes, she climbed the stairs and knocked on the commanding double door—bright pink, of course.

Within moments, Rick opened the door and stood with a kitchen towel over one shoulder. He wore khaki shorts and a blue shirt that brought out his eye color. He looked startlingly handsome and every bit the movie star.

"Hey, Whitney. You look nice." He stepped back. "Come on in."

She followed him inside, taking in the understated but elegant beach decor. Someone with a great eye for interior design had furnished the house. There were cool mint green chairs, a white sofa that begged to be sat on, and soft, flowing curtains on the side windows. A huge wall of windows and French doors covered the entire back wall of the house, with a stunning view of the bay. "This place is lovely."

"My grandmother likes it. She comes here often." Rick continued on until they reached the kitchen.

The great room in the back and the kitchen were all one flowing room, perfect for entertaining. She couldn't imagine renting a place this grand, and it boggled her mind Rick's family had rented *two* houses like this for *two full weeks*. He looked right at home in the place, though. He moved with a self-confident ease.

She wondered if he'd like to share some of that ease with her…

He walked to the enormous fridge and pulled open the door. "I have another bottle of white burgundy. You seemed to enjoy that last night. But I also have beer. Or there is red wine over on the bar."

Trying not to seem overwhelmed by the house, the fact she was once again having dinner with a famous actor, or the choices of beverages, she slowly walked farther into the kitchen. "I'll just have a beer, if that's okay."

"Of course." He stood back a step. "Take your pick."

She looked in the refrigerator. It held a dizzying

array of bottled beer, most of which she didn't recognize. "I'll have a Corona." She at least recognized that bottle.

He reached for the beer and then snagged one of the fancy named bottles for himself. He got out two glasses from the tall cabinets perched over the expansive granite countertop. She watched his hands as he expertly sliced a lime and poured her beer. He gave her a glass and raised his own. "Here's to a non-eventful dinner."

She'd drink to that.

Rick grabbed a tray with their steaks and led the way out onto the deck. "It's a nice evening. I thought we'd sit outside while I barbecue."

Whitney followed him outside and settled into the glider near the grill. He put the steaks on and sat next to her, close enough to touch her and smell a hint of her perfume.

She took a sip of her beer. "The view here is gorgeous. I bet you see some fabulous sunsets."

"I've caught a few since I've gotten here. They are nice."

"The bay is so wide here, you can barely see the shore across the way."

"My grandmother says she loves to sit right out here on this glider when she stays here. Of course, she brings a cook and her assistant with her when she comes."

"Really?"

He grinned. "At least. Sometimes more."

"I can't even imagine."

"My grandmother thinks I'm roughing it this week with no cook or other help."

"I guess you didn't tell her about eating at Sweet Caroline's every day." She smiled at him. "But you did say that you're a grilling whiz."

"Just you wait. The steaks will be great."

She looked at him doubtfully. "Somehow I don't picture you as a chef."

"Well, I can grill. That's about it." He shrugged. "I'm also a whiz at heating up leftovers in the microwave."

"A man of many talents."

He felt his phone vibrate, and he took it out of his pocket. Shawna again.

"You can get that if you need to." She nodded at his phone.

"Nah, it's not important." He slid the phone back into his pocket. No way was he having the conversation he needed to have with Shawna while Whitney was sitting here right next to him. He still was a bit surprised—and proud of himself—for convincing Whitney to come over.

"So you said you grew up in Philadelphia." She sipped her beer and looked at him with her endless blue eyes.

Focus on words, not eyes. "Yes, mostly. I went to a private school, then I went away to camp each summer. My parents were really busy." Really, really busy. Sometimes he wondered why they'd had kids. Well, except now they got to brag about his sister the surgeon and his brother the lawyer. "How about you? I bet you grew up in a house with a white picket fence and family dinners."

She looked out at the bay. "Not exactly." Her voice was soft and low. "My mother died when I was a young girl."

"I'm sorry. I shouldn't have just blurted out my imagined perfect life for you." He was a clueless fool.

She nodded, accepting his apology. "My father didn't handle it well. He—my father—was gone a lot after that. He would just—disappear."

"That must have been tough."

He watched her take a slow sip of beer, then square her shoulders. "My brother basically raised me from then on. He took multiple jobs, dropped out of school at one point to work to keep food on our table. We kept it a secret that my father was gone so often."

"I can't even imagine, I'm sorry."

"Well, we did okay, though I was always afraid that someone would come and take me away. I was afraid they'd come and throw me in an orphanage or foster home."

He was never again going to complain about his childhood. His was a bed of roses compared to hers. "So do you ever see your father now?"

"I do. He came back a year or so ago. We made peace with our past. He's a good man and regrets he wasn't there for us back then. But Willie and I turned out okay."

"You're close to your brother. He accepts you for the person you are. I envy you being that close to him."

"You're close with your grandmother."

"I am. I adore her."

"And your nieces."

"But not my siblings."

"Families are strange things, aren't they?" She trailed a finger through the moisture on her glass, lost in thought, then her delicate fingers wrapped around her drink.

He couldn't quit sneaking quick looks over at her. She'd found a lot of forgiveness in her heart. He admired her for that. Heck, he admired her for so many things. Like the fact they could sit here and talk like this and he wasn't afraid she was just looking for a story she could later tell about on social media.

Whitney insisted on helping clean up the dishes after dinner. It was the least she could do after he cooked this meal for her. Even if he did kind of burn the steaks, not that she let on she thought that. He seemed so proud of his grilling whiz title.

They puttered in the kitchen, loading the dishwasher and putting leftovers in the fridge.

"I could drive you home."

"No, that's not necessary."

"Then how about I walk you home? I don't feel comfortable letting you walk back home alone." He set a towel on the counter.

"You realize I walk home alone every night." She rolled her eyes.

"But I asked you over. This is different." He winked at her. "It was hard enough to say yes when you said not to come pick you up. But I'd just convinced you to come to dinner, so I didn't want to push my luck."

"Well, if it will make *you* feel better, then you can walk me back home." Might as well humor him.

"It will."

"Well, we must always be about what makes *you* feel better," she teased him.

They walked outside and down the long stairway. The evening sky dazzled them with starlight. They headed toward her house, and he tucked her hand on his elbow. She left it there, enjoying his closeness as they fell into step. They chatted more about the weather forecast for the party and his growing to-do list.

"I usually have someone who handles this kind of planning for me." He shrugged. "But I wanted to do this myself, for my grandmother."

"I'm sure whatever you do, however the party turns out, she'll love it."

He walked her up to her door. She debated asking him in. She needed to get up early in the morning but wasn't ready for the evening to end.

"You going to invite me in?" He put on a proper pretty-please look.

She laughed. "Yes, of course. You did walk me all the way across town."

"I did. It was… exhausting. I should probably sit with you for a while until I'm all rested up."

"Of course, you should." Her heart did a tiny flip, which was ridiculous. He'd just been polite to walk her home. She was just being polite asking him in.

She unlocked the door, led him through the house, and out on the back deck. They stood at the edge of the deck, enjoying the gentle sea breeze. She looked up at the starlit sky and suddenly a silly thought popped into her mind. "So… why do you think they call actors movie stars? I mean, I wonder how the term star got started. Who decided actors were *stars*?"

"I never really thought about it. Though, there are other stars, right? Like baseball star, country music star?"

"I guess you're right. It's all you glittery, shiny people."

"Not sure I've been called glittery before."

"You know what I mean." She looked at him, leaning against the deck rail, all relaxed. *Just like a regular person.* Only he wasn't a regular person. He was a movie star.

He looked down at her then, with his make-her-knees-go-weak-like-a-fool smile. He stood for a moment, looking at her. "Have you ever been kissed by a glittery person before?"

"I—"

She felt him, more than saw him, lean toward her to kiss her. Time froze. The heat from his body spread through her. But he was a *movie star*. His eyes were filled with... With what? Her thoughts collided in her brain. Uncertainty twisted with longing. Fear—not of him, but of her feelings—washed through her. At the last second, she turned her head, and he brushed a kiss on her cheek.

He stepped away and tossed her an impish grin. "Close enough." He took her hand in his. "I had a really great time tonight."

She tried to concentrate on words, not the almost-kiss. "I did, too." The warmth of his hand spread through her, connecting her with him. She didn't think she ever wanted him to let go of her hand. Which was ridiculous. She barely knew the man, right? Oh, the confusion he caused.

"I should go." He looked down at her hand in his.

She nodded. He let her hand slip out of his, walked down the stairs, and with one last smile, disappeared around the cottage.

She stood on the deck, her now empty, lonely hand resting on the railing. She looked out to sea with the waves rolling to shore in a relentless march. She looked up at the endless, starlit sky, suddenly feeling all alone and small standing here beside the ocean.

What kind of trouble had she gotten herself into now?

## CHAPTER 9

The next morning, Rick grabbed his phone off the table when it rang insistently. Shawna again. He couldn't keep ignoring her forever. Though... maybe he could. He set the phone down without answering. A tiny bit of guilt hovered over him for ignoring her. Again. He'd talk to her soon, but right now, he needed to work on the birthday party. That was his number one priority.

*Or, he could admit he was just flat out avoiding Shawna...*

And another thing. He needed to quit thinking about his near-kiss with Whitney. He'd been surprised when she'd ducked her head at the last minute, not that he blamed her. He'd caused her nothing but trouble with the photos and people in town talking about her.

He looked at his to-to list, the kiss firmly out of his mind. Kinda. He decided to confirm everything with the musicians he'd hired. He tapped in their phone number. A squeaking recording came on. "I'm sorry, the number you called is no longer in service."

He looked at his notes again and confirmed he'd put in the correct number. He scowled, then took out his laptop, opened his browser window, and searched the internet for the website of the band. Before he could locate it, a notification for his social media account flashed across his screen. He clicked on it and sat back in his chair.

Whitney's name was plastered all over social media. Someone had obviously given her name to the press. He clicked over to a Hollywood gossip site and saw a video of a reporter interviewing Shawna. He clicked on the sound and sat back while Shawna, in the way only Shawna could make everything all about her, tell the reporter Whitney's name.

He was torn between calling Shawna and letting loose on her—she knew how much he valued his privacy—and rushing over to let Whitney know her secret was out. Of course, he had to admit, he'd ignored Shawna's calls for days.

He slammed the laptop shut. He'd better go talk to Whitney. She was not going to be pleased.

He grabbed his keys and headed out the door. He glanced at the red sports car. It turned a lot of heads wherever it went, but at least he'd get to Coastal Creations more quickly. The faster he got there, the faster... she'd kill him. He sighed. He needed to get to the shop before Whitney found out from anyone else. He had to try to make this right.

Whitney sat behind the counter at Coastal Creations working on the necklace for Viola Lemmons. It was turning out nicely, which pleased her. She didn't know why she felt so much pressure to assure that this piece was special.

She shook her head. Of course she knew why she was so attached to this piece. She wanted Rick to be proud of her work. She reached up and touched her face, a gesture that she'd done about a hundred times since he'd kissed her cheek last night.

Oh, she knew he'd been going for her lips, but she'd been so taken by surprise that she'd turned her head at the last moment and he'd pressed a kiss to her cheek.

The cheek she kept touching. A blush warmed her face from the memory of the look in the depths of his deep blue eyes.

Luckily, she hadn't fallen for the magnetic draw of those eyes of his.

*She hadn't.*

She didn't want to be a weekend fling. Not with Rick. Not with anyone. He had a life across the country. She had one here. Besides, Willie had said Rick was involved with Shawna Jacobson. Though, maybe he was used to dating several women at once.

What did she know about the glamorous Hollywood life?

She had to admit, she'd been just the tiniest bit sorry she hadn't let him kiss her properly. Though, maybe he was just going to give her a friendly peck on the lips.

She set the necklace down in frustration. Why, oh why, did she always have the tendency to overthink things? She looked up at the sound of the bell jangling over the door.

"Miss Layton?" A man entered the shop.

Great. A customer would take her mind off things. Specifically, Rick. "Yes, may I help you?"

"I'm Steve Jones from the Charleston Review. I wanted to know if you have a statement about your relationship with Rick Nichols."

She grabbed the edge of the counter. "My what?"

"Your relationship with Rick Nichols. What is it like to date a movie star? Did you ever think you'd meet someone like him in Indigo Bay?" The Steve guy hammered out questions.

"I don't have a relationship with Rick Nichols."

"But you had dinner with him at Bistro Fifty. You've been seen around town with him."

"I…" She looked up when the bell above the door rang again, then she grabbed the counter even tighter. *This was not going to help.* "Rick…"

The reporter whirled around. "Mr. Nichols. Steve Jones here from the Charleston Review. Would you like to make a statement about your relationship with Miss Layton?"

"What I'd like is for you to leave the shop." Rick's eyes flashed with fury. "There's no reason to invade Miss Layton's privacy or to bother her at her place of work."

"I just wanted to get—"

"You were just leaving." He held the door open.

The reporter held his ground for a moment, then sighed and slipped past Rick and out the door. He stood outside on the sidewalk though, refusing to leave.

Rick grabbed his cell phone. "Mitchell, I need a detail, pronto. Indigo Bay, South Carolina. Twenty-four-hour coverage. I expect you here by evening. Yes, thank you."

Rick walked over to her. "You okay?" His voice was low and soothing.

It did nothing to subdue her nerves. She released her grip on the counter and sank onto the stool.

"Whitney, you look… frazzled."

"Frazzled? This is *frazzled*? This is certifiably upset."

"I was on my way to tell you that your name got out. I was hoping to tell you—"

"Before I found out by a reporter waylaying me in my shop?"

"Um, yes, before that." He walked behind the counter and put a hand on her shoulder. "I'm so sorry."

"How can I run my shop if reporters and media people hang around outside my door? How do I know who's coming in to order some of my jewelry and who's just a looky-loo trying to see Rick Nichols' new conquest?"

"You're not a conquest."

"What am I?" She looked him right in the eyes.

"I…" A sheepish look covered his face. "I don't know what we are. I like you. I enjoy your company. You're fun to be with. You don't ever treat me like—"

"Like what?"

"Like an actor. Someone you only want to be with because of what I am." He dropped his hand from her shoulder.

She sat in stunned silence. She hadn't even thought about all of this from *his* angle. How he never knew if someone was interested in Rick the person or Rick the actor. She looked closely at him again and slowly took his hand in hers. "I never thought of it like that, from your perspective. I just keep thinking, why is someone like you going out with someone like me?"

"Because you're kind, and pretty, and have a quick smile. Because I enjoy being around you. Because you like to watch sunsets and you didn't even mention that I burned the steaks last night."

She laughed then, and the laughter freed the tension coursing through her. "They *were* possibly a tad overcooked."

"They were burnt. I got so involved talking to you that I didn't watch them carefully enough."

"The salad was good, though. And the dessert." She smiled.

"The salad came from a bag… and I got the pie from Sweet Caroline's."

She laughed again. "I knew the pie was from Caroline's, but I wasn't going to let on that I knew."

"But I kept my promise about no reporters or photos."

"You did. At least *last night*…" She tossed him a wry smile.

Rick watched as some of the tension slowly drained from Whitney. Her shoulders relaxed, and she smiled at him. But she was right. This was going to make running her business a nightmare. He looked down at her small hand holding his. As if she could read his thoughts, she withdrew her hand and it took all his restraint not to snatch it back in his.

He scrubbed his now-free hand across his jaw. "I'm sorry about all of this, but I've taken care of things."

Her eyes narrowed. "What did you do, exactly?"

"Well, I've hired some… *people* to help out with that whole reporter-photographer problem."

"You did what?" Her narrowed eyes flew open wide, their sky-blue tones darkening.

"I have some men who will be outside your shop and your house. A female will be with you here in the shop. She can pretend to be a worker here if that's better for you.

"You've hired *bodyguards* for me?"

"Well, not exactly." He delicately sidestepped the question.

She stood up and faced him, toe to toe. "Then what would *you* call them?"

"A security detail?" He carefully watched her face.

"So… bodyguards."

He sighed. "Yes, bodyguards. Just until this blows over."

"And how long do you think it will take until this *blows over*?"

He reached up and massaged his temples. "Something else will come along that catches the media's eye. It always does."

"Somehow, that isn't very comforting."

"I'm sorry about all of this."

"I do *not* want someone following me around all the time."

The door flung open, and a woman rushed in. "Miss Layton, Mr. Nichols."

A flash blinded him for a minute. He sprang forward and took the woman's arm. "Out."

"I just want…"

"Out of the shop." He pushed her out the door and locked it behind her.

"You can't lock the door. You'll lock out my customers." A look of panic crossed Whitney's face.

"I know. The only solution I can come up with is hiring my security detail until things settle down."

Her shoulders slumped, and she sank back onto the stool. "I guess you're right."

"I'll stay here today and fend off reporters." He gave her a small smile. "I'll be your doorman. How does that sound?"

"It sounds… crazy."

"But it will work, won't it? Until the security people get here?"

"I don't think having Rick Nichols answering the door to my shop is really going to help the problem, will it?"

He scowled. He hadn't thought of it that way. "No, probably not."

She sighed. "I guess I'll close the shop for the rest of the day."

"I don't want you losing money on my account." He rubbed a hand over his jaw.

"I'll work on your grandmother's necklace. At least I can do that much."

She slowly walked over to the door and flipped the sign so it said closed. "I'm going to take this to the backroom and work on it." She gathered up a cloth that held the necklace.

"I'm staying with you."

"You don't have to."

"I'm staying until my people show up, just in case."

"Have it your way." She shrugged, and he

followed her to the backroom. A large window allowed light to flood onto a big table that held an array of wires, gems, shells, and sea glass. The items were spilled across the table in a haphazard manner. How did she ever find what she was looking for? He didn't dare voice his question, though. She was aggravated enough with him.

He took a stool, perched at the end of the table, and watched her work. She bit her lip as she carefully wrapped a wire around the piece of sea glass, creating a beautiful swirl of silver around the glass. He stared in fascination as she lost herself in her artistry.

He looked at his watch and was surprised it was already a little after noon. Whitney sat up straight and tilted her head from side to side.

He got up and walked to stand behind her. He put his hands on her shoulders and slowly started to massage the knots out of her muscles.

"I'd purr if I could." Her voice was low.

His fingers pushed and prodded and coaxed her shoulders to relax. The fresh scent of her shampoo filled the air surrounding her. He wanted to lean down and kiss her head, spin her around, kiss her…

But he wasn't quite ready for her to turn her cheek to him again.

∼

She tried not to focus on Rick's warm, firm hands on her shoulders. Her body warred with the decision to relax under his careful, tender massage or to tense up because his body was right behind her, inches away.

She gave in and lost herself in his touch, feeling the stress of the morning and the tension of concentrating on her work melt away under his touch.

He stopped, and she had to bite her lip to keep from begging him to keep going. He slowly spun her stool to turn her to face him.

She knew, *just knew*, he was going to kiss her.

"If I kiss you again, are you going to duck your head?" He whispered the words.

She shook her head no, unable to speak or concentrate on anything other than his tender voice and his lips headed for hers.

He tilted her chin up and lowered his lips to meet hers. She didn't know what she was expecting... fireworks, music, a marching band. But instead, a feeling of rightness came over her. Like his lips should be on hers, and he should have his hand gently resting on her cheek. He slowly and deliberately pulled her to her feet and kissed her again, wrapping both his arms around her, pulling her close. She leaned against him and heard a small moan escape her lips.

He pulled back slightly and tossed a lazy, movie-star smile at her. "That's more like it."

He leaned closer again, and she closed her eyes, waiting for another kiss, wanting another kiss. The sound of a phone ringing jarred through the room, and he pulled away, snatching away the kiss she so badly wanted.

"I better get that." He took a step back and snagged his phone.

"Shawna, hey."

She stood there, lost, waiting for the second kiss that hadn't happened while Rick answered a phone call from his *girlfriend*.

# CHAPTER 10

Rick sent Whitney a rueful look. "I'll just go take this in the other room."

She just nodded.

He strode to the front room, closing the door to the backroom on his way.

Shawna's voice came clearly across the airways. "Rick, I've been trying to get ahold of you for days. I've left messages. You haven't answered them. Haven't called me back."

"What the heck were you doing giving Whitney's name to that reporter?" He interrupted her litany of his shortcomings.

"What? Well... I didn't think it was any big secret."

"You could have asked."

"I *tried* to talk to you," she accused him.

He reached up and rubbed his shoulder. She had. He'd ignored her.

"You know I like to keep my private life private."

"Well, I didn't think it was really anything serious between you and that Whitney woman, anyway. I mean she's a... shop owner. You're, well, you're an actor."

Rick bristled at her words. "You're such a snob sometimes."

"*Nice.*" Her brittle word chastised him.

He sighed. "I'm sorry. I'm stressed dealing with all of this."

"Why don't you come home?" Her voice wheedled him.

"You know I can't. I have the party for Grandmere to plan." That reminded him. He still needed to deal with the band.

"You could hire people to do that. What do you know about planning a party?"

"I'm doing just fine with it."

"But that's silly. Let me call my event coordinator for you. She'll finish everything up. You can just show up for the party. Anyway, there's a big party here in L.A. this weekend. I'd love for you to go with me. You could still get back for your grandmother's party. My agent called and said it would be good for us to be seen together. It might help with this new movie we're hoping to get. You do still want the lead role in it, don't you?"

"Yes, of course, I do." But did he? Sometimes he wondered what it would be like to break out of his typical role and try something different.

"Good, because you're acting… odd."

"But I can't leave, especially not for some publicity stunt your agent wants. And no, this party is something I want to do for Grandmere. I don't want your coordinator to plan something. She'd have no idea what my grandmother likes."

"You're so stubborn about the strangest things." He could hear the irritation in her voice.

"I've gotta go." He'd deal with her later.

"Next time how about answering my calls?"

"Bye, Shawna." He clicked off the phone and shoved it in his pocket. Sometimes she could be the most irksome person he knew even if she was mainly harmless.

Whitney ignored Rick when he came back. If Shawna calling hadn't given her a big dose of reality, she didn't know what would. She kept her head bent over her work.

He walked over to the table and put a hand on her shoulder. She jumped up off the stool. "I need to take a break. I'm going to go get lunch."

"Great. Where do you want to go?"

"I think I'll run home. I'll catch up with you later."

"I'm not letting you go home alone."

Who did he think he was? Telling her that he wasn't going to *let* her go home. "I'm going. I'm hungry." She had to go, put some distance between them.

He let out a long, deep breath. "Look, there will probably be reporters at your home."

"No." Her hand flew to her throat. "Not at my house. How?"

"Everyone in town knows where you live. It won't take them long to find out."

"I can't… I can't live like this." Her pulse raced. Where would she be safe from all the prying eyes and flashes of cameras? Where would she be safe from Rick? The man with the girlfriend who'd just called him.

"As soon as my security people get here—"

"As soon as they get here I get to have people follow me around all the time? I get no privacy?"

"Whitney, I'm so sorry."

"So you said." She glared at him. Why did he mess with her anyway when he was obviously seeing Shawna? Maybe it was just some silly game with him. Well, it wasn't a game to her.

He frowned. "Did I do something wrong? I mean, besides the obvious fact the reporters are here because of me?"

Her phone rang, and she crossed over to the counter to pick it up, annoyed at the interruption because she was ready to tell Rick exactly what was wrong with this situation. In excruciating detail.

"Is everything okay?" Merry's anxious voice filtered through the phone. "I came by the shop and you were closed. You never close your shop. Not during the busy season. And there were all these people hanging around outside."

"Those would be reporters. It appears my name is now forever linked to Rick's." She glared at him again for good measure.

"I'm sorry. I'd hoped it would just blow over for you. I know how you hate attention like this. So you had to close the shop?"

"For today. Then it appears that I get bodyguards to keep the reporters away."

"For real?" She couldn't miss the incredulous tone in Merry's voice.

"It appears so. I'm not amused."

Rick paced back and forth across the expanse of the room while she talked. He chewed his lip, then reached up to rub his shoulder.

"Can I do anything to help?"

"Well, I'm starving and it seems I'm not *allowed* to go home for lunch." She tossed the words out as much for Merry as for Rick. He stopped his pacing, looked at her, and frowned.

"I'll bring you something from Sweet Caroline's."

"Honestly, that would be great if you don't mind. Are you sure?" Her stomach growled in anticipation.

"Yep, I'll be there in a jif."

"Thanks, you're the best."

∾

Whitney drew the blinds firmly on all her windows that evening. She couldn't even leave them open so she could sit and look out at the ocean. Rick had wanted to come in after he'd introduced her to Mitch, who it appeared would be her new constant companion. She'd told Rick she was tired and closed the door on him. Okay, more like slammed the door on him. He could take his bewildered look and go back to The Pink Ladies. Maybe his rental would be surrounded by reporters, too. Let him deal with the chaos.

Mitch had sent the reporters off her property and settled down on a chair on her front porch after taking a quick look around the outside of the cottage. He seemed a nice enough guy. She was just creeped out by thinking people were trying to spy on her and grab a photo at any time.

A quick knock at her door stopped her in her tracks. "Miss Layton, it's Mitch."

She crossed over and cracked the door open. "Yes?"

"There's a Merry here to see you. She said if I didn't knock and say she was here, she was going to start screaming your name…"

She cracked a small smile. "Yes, Merry is always welcome here."

"I'll remember that, ma'am."

Merry pushed past him, her arms laden with packages. "I brought dinner. And wine. And you get me for company for dinner. Lasagna for the meal. Chocolate cake for dessert."

She took a tote from Merry's arms. "I'm so glad to see you. I'm going crazy in my locked-down, buttoned-up cottage."

"There's nothing that good old lasagna can't fix. Well, especially if followed by chocolate and accompanied by wine. Go sit down and I'll reheat this. Tell me all about your day. Everything. We barely got to talk when I brought you lunch. I could see the icy daggers you were tossing at Rick. What happened?"

Whitney sank onto a kitchen chair, placed her elbows on the table, and rested her chin on her palms. "I'm such a fool."

Merry turned on the oven and slid the lasagna in. She poured them both a glass of white wine and sat across from Whitney. "Okay, now tell me everything."

"I... well, this reporter came into the shop this morning and snapped my photo and started rattling off all these questions. I was so surprised. Then Rick came in. Then another reporter. Then somehow Rick set up that I'd have a security detail. Me. A *security detail.*" She shook her head.

"So that's why you're so mad at him?" Merry's eyes narrowed. "It's not really his fault, is it?"

"It's not just that. I knew he was an actor when I went to dinner with him. Didn't realize just how popular he was or how the media might turn my life upside down."

Merry took a sip of her wine and sat watching her.

Whitney let out a long sigh. "It's... he kissed me."

"You're mad at him because he kissed you?"

"No. Well, yes. I am. And I'm mad at myself because I *let* him kiss me."

"Because you don't want to be involved with an actor?"

"Not just that. I don't want to be involved with an actor who is seeing someone else." She set her glass down with a little too much force and wine splashed onto the table.

Merry popped up, grabbed a towel, and swiped at the spill. "Is he seeing someone else?"

"Willie said the rumors are that he's seeing Shawna Jacobson. And guess who called right after Rick kissed me?"

"No. Shawna did?"

"Yep. And he got up and took the call in the other room." She buried her face in her hands. "I'm a fool. I'm just someone for him to amuse himself with while he's in town. I thought... well, we've talked a lot and I've enjoyed his company."

"So you like him?"

"No. Well, I thought maybe I liked him a little. Maybe. Then he kissed me and I got a little lost in him. That's silly, isn't it? He's a movie star, for Pete's sake. I'm... well, I'm just me."

"You're a fabulous, smart, talented, beautiful woman. He'd be lucky to have you."

She threw a thankful look at Merry. "You'll always be my biggest fan, won't you?"

"I am. But I'm telling the truth."

"Well, it doesn't matter, because he has a girlfriend."

"Are you sure?"

Whitney nodded her head. "I'm sure Willie is right. He said there are lots of photos of them together online. I should never have…"

"What? You should never have let yourself kiss a guy you were attracted to?"

"I should have known better. Now I'm in this mess with bodyguards and I'm not sure how this will affect my business." She took a sip of the pinot grigio, savoring the crisp, familiar tones of her favorite brand. At least some things were the same in her world. Merry coming to her rescue, her favorite meal warming in the oven, and the taste of her best-loved wine.

"I'm sorry." Merry reached across the table and squeezed Whitney's hand. "What are you going to do now?"

"I'm going to avoid him and count the days until he leaves Indigo Bay."

## CHAPTER 11

Whitney rolled over in bed and grabbed her phone from the nightstand, fighting off the haze of sleep. "Hello?"

"Hey, sis."

"Willie, what time is it?"

"You sleeping in today?"

She opened her eyes and glanced at the clock. She sat straight up in bed. "Overslept." She was going to have to rush around to get the shop open on time. Then it all came rushing back.

Rick's kiss.

Bodyguards.

Ugh.

"I thought you said you and that Rick Nichols had nothing going between you."

"We don't." They didn't. Not anymore. And she'd make sure of that from now on. She slid out of bed and crossed over to her closet.

"Yet, there you are, kissing the guy."

"What are you talking about?"

"A photo of you and Rick kissing. It's all over social media. You even hit the Indigo Bay news section on their website, not to mention the Charleston Review."

"What?" She paused, her hand still on the doorknob of the closet door.

"You're kissing that Rick guy. Looks like the photo was taken in the back room of your shop."

"But how?"

Willie sighed. "Whit, get a grip. You awake? Looks like they took it through the window with a telephoto lens."

"They can't do that, can they?" She walked back across the room and sank onto the bed.

"Maybe not, but they did, even though I think it's kind of creepy."

"I can't believe they'd do that. It's so invasive. Don't I have any right to privacy?"

"Probably not if you're dating a movie star."

"I'm not *dating* him."

"Okay, if you're *kissing* a movie star."

She didn't miss the sarcastic tone in his voice. "It's all such a mess, Willie. I'm a fool. You know what happened right after that kiss? Shawna Jacobson called him."

"You want me to come and set the guy straight?" The brotherly overprotectiveness was somehow comforting, and she was tempted to tell him yes.

But she could take care of this herself. "No, I've got it handled. I won't make the same mistake."

"Well, you know I'll be there in no time if you need me."

"Thanks, but I'm fine. It will all blow over soon."

She hung up the phone with the tightly closed blinds that usually let the morning sunrise filter into her room mocking her. She pushed off the bed and wandered through the silent, lonely, dark house to grab a cup of coffee, dreading what else the day had to offer up in surprises.

Rick left yet another message on Whitney's phone. He wasn't sure why she wasn't taking his call. She'd acted strangely all yesterday afternoon. He'd gotten her all set up with the security detail, then she'd basically closed her door in his face. He didn't know if it was because of all the attention, the bodyguards, or because he'd kissed her.

A very nice kiss, in his opinion.

*Don't go there. Get back to work on the party.*

He frowned and stared at his to-do list. He'd found another phone number for the band and left a message, as well as contacting them through their website. He was *sure* he'd hear back from them today. Positive.

He'd checked with the caterer who assured him everything was under control. At least that was one aspect of the party that wasn't going sideways on him. He knocked on the wooden table after he had that thought... just in case.

He got up and poured himself another cup of coffee and went out onto the deck to enjoy the morning sunshine. So far he'd seen no sign of reporters around The Pink Ladies, but he'd no doubt they'd show up soon. He had another security detail coming today to keep reporters and onlookers away from the rentals, though he was sure his grandmother and her party would attract a large array of media attention. But for now, he'd enjoy his coffee in peace.

Except for the fact that Whitney didn't answer his calls last night or this morning...

He wanted to go talk to her, but showing up at her work would cause more trouble for her, which was the last thing he wanted to do.

Yet, he needed to talk to her.

But right now, her needs were more important to him than his own.

With ball cap and sunglasses firmly in place, Rick headed into town to grab lunch at Sweet Caroline's. Not that he hoped he'd run into Whitney there... but then it wouldn't be him going to see her and causing problems, it would just be a nice... coincidence.

By the time he'd finished his meal, there was no sign of Whitney. She was probably hiding out in her shop. He'd already called Mitch four times today to check on her. The man was probably going to start avoiding his calls, too.

He glanced up as someone planted themselves in front of his table. "Merry, hi."

"Rick."

He wasn't sure if anyone could put more ice into a single word.

"How's Whitney today? She's not taking my calls."

Merry snorted. "No kidding."

"I know she's upset about all the publicity."

"You mean like the photo of your kiss plastered all over social media?"

"Our kiss?"

"Didn't you see it today? Someone creeped you two and took a photo of you kissing her. It's all over the news. I bet your girlfriend isn't too happy about that."

"My girlfriend?" Whitney's friend wasn't making much sense.

"Your girlfriend. Shawna Jacobson."

"Shawna's not my girlfriend."

Merry raised an eyebrow. "Oh, really?"

"Seriously. It's all just publicity stuff with Shawna. Our agents think it helps. It does help, I guess. But there's nothing going on between the two of us."

Merry narrowed her eyes, searching his face. "If that's the truth, you need to talk to Whitney."

"I'm *trying* to. She won't answer my calls."

"I'll tell you what. I'll set up a meeting with her

where there won't be any prying eyes. But I'm warning you. If you end up hurting Whit, you're going to answer to me." Merry spun around and disappeared out of the restaurant.

Rick snuck in the back door to Merry's house with the key that was under the clay kitten on her back step, just like she said. Did people really keep keys hidden under something on their steps these days? He had two separate locks on his door in Los Angeles.

He closed the door behind him and walked into her house. He'd made sure no one was following him. He went around to the windows and pulled the blinds as they'd discussed.

Now, if Merry could just get Whitney to come to her house, he'd get a chance to talk to her. He paced the floor for what seemed like hours. A big clock on the wall clicked as the minutes ticked by. He wished he could throw a book at it to silence it once and for all.

He continued his pacing back and forth, then to change things up, he went around in a circular path around the edge of the rug.

He glared at the deafening clock again. It must be broken because it assured him that only five minutes had passed since he'd entered the room. He'd talk to Merry about that. How *did* the woman stand the noise?

Tick. Tock. Tick. Tock.

He heard voices outside, stepped over to the window, and gently slid the slats on the blinds apart, just wide enough so he could peek outside. Merry, Whitney, and the ever-present Mitch stood on the front porch. A few reporters lurked in the street but stayed back when Mitch turned and shooed them away with threats of calling the police if they came onto private property.

"Come on in." Merry's voice filtered through the door, and he heard the sound of a key in the lock. He stepped away from the window and stood waiting.

Waiting to see if Whitney would talk to him.

Waiting to see if she'd believe him.

## CHAPTER 12

Whitney clutched Merry's arm when she saw Rick standing in the living room. "What are you doing here?"

"I just wanted to talk to you."

"How did you get in here?"

"I…" He looked at Merry.

Whitney turned to stare at her. "Did you know he was here? Of course you did. That's why you wouldn't take no for an answer when you invited me over."

"I think you should listen to what he has to say." Merry turned and walked toward the kitchen. "I'm going to make some tea. Or, you know, do something. You two talk."

*Since when did Merry desert her when she needed her?*

Whitney took one more step into the room but made sure to keep her distance from Rick. "I'm not sure we have anything to say."

"I think we do. Will you please just listen to me?" He took a step closer and reached out toward her.

She couldn't help herself, she took a quick step backward.

He stopped and put his hands in his pockets. "I didn't know what happened after I kissed you. I thought that... well, that kiss meant something to me. But you walled me out. I know I brought all this chaos into your life. I am sorry about that. But... it seems I care about you, Whitney. You're funny, charming, talented and I've enjoyed my time with you these last few days more than I've enjoyed spending time with someone in a very long time." He paused and frowned. "A *really* long time. Like forever. I feel a connection to you. You make me smile when I'm just thinking about you."

Whitney crossed over to the sofa, her hand gripping the arm of it to steady herself as she lowered herself onto it. Her heart pounded in her chest at Rick's words and the look in his eyes. His eyes said he was telling the truth.

Her mind reminded her that he was an actor.

He came over and sat beside her. "I know that Shawna called and interrupted us. I'm not involved with her no matter what you see on social media. It's all just publicity. Directors like to hire us for what they believe is the chemistry between us. But I don't feel that way about her, not at all. She's a coworker, that is all."

She looked deep into his steel blue eyes, wanting

to believe him. All she could see was sincerity and truth in their depths.

He reached out and took her hand in his. The heat of his touch scorched through her, a lightning bolt of connection.

He sat, waiting for her reaction, her answer to his words.

She took a deep breath and a huge leap of faith. "Kiss me again."

At the sound of a knock at the door, Whitney reluctantly pulled away from Rick's kiss. He growled the tiniest bit as she pulled back. She did so love his growls.

Merry hurried into the room. "Austin texted me. He's here." She grinned at Whitney.

Whitney scooted away from Rick as Merry went to answer the door.

"What's up with the guy at the door and why did he have to check if I could come inside?" Austin stepped into the room and gave Merry a quick kiss.

"That's Whitney's bodyguard." Merry laughed.

Austin looked over at her, then Rick. His eyes widened in recognition. "Hey, aren't you Rick Nichols?"

Rick nodded.

"Honey, where have you been?" Merry took Austin's arm and led him into the room. "Have you not seen the coverage? Whit and Rick are the new hot item."

"Not funny, Mere." She scowled at her friend.

Merry just grinned. "I swear, both you and Austin are so non-techie, non-social media inclined. Don't know what you two would do without me."

Austin wrapped his arm around Merry's waist. "I don't know what I'd do without you either." He winked at her.

Rick stood up and held out his hand. "I'm Rick, as you've already figured out."

"Austin Sullivan." The men shook hands as they eyed each other in that way that males have of sizing each other up.

"So, how about I go grab us some beers and we can relax for a while?" Merry asked.

"I'll help." Whitney jumped up and followed Merry into the kitchen.

"So, did you two work things out?" Merry opened the fridge door.

"I think so. He says he's not involved with Shawna, that she's just a co-worker."

"And you believe him?"

"I do. I mean, why would he lie to me? And his eyes said he was telling the truth."

"I thought he was, too. I ran into him at Sweet Caroline's. That's why I invited you both over. So you would have a chance to talk without the media around. You can thank me now, or thank me later." Merry grinned.

"You're the best friend in the world. Will that do for thanks?"

"That'll do." Merry handed her two bottles of beer, and they walked back into the front room.

Rick had settled back on the sofa and she walked over, sat down, and handed him his drink.

"So, what brings you to Indigo Bay?" Austin sat in a chair across from them.

"I'm planning a birthday party for my grandmother."

"His grandmother is Viola Lemmons," Merry explained.

Austin frowned.

"Viola Lemmons. Movie star." Merry shook her head. "Really, both you and Whit are a full-time job, just explaining the world to you."

"Oh, right. The actress."

"Rick is staying at The Pink Ladies. He's having the party there," Whitney explained.

"Do you have everything settled for the party?" Merry perched on the arm of Austin's chair.

"Almost. Except for the band. I can't seem to get ahold of them to confirm everything, which is strange because he was very communicative when I first booked him." He took a sip of his beer and leaned back on the sofa, stretching out his long legs. One of his legs rested against hers, sending waves of warmth through her. And a desire for him to kiss her again.

"What band did you hire?" Merry asked.

"The Gary Simpson Band."

"Oh, no." Merry jumped up.

"Oh no, what?" A frown creased Rick's face.

"Gary was in an accident a couple of weeks ago. He's in the hospital. Another guy from his band was hurt, too."

Rick set his beer on the coffee table and ran his hand through his hair. "So, I guess they won't be playing at the party." He reached up and rubbed his neck. "What else can go wrong? I really don't seem to have much luck with this party planning stuff."

"I know a DJ you could use. Danny. He does all kinds of music and he's got a good, charming patter of conversation in between songs. If he's available, I bet he'd do a great job for you." Whitney took her phone out of her pocket. "You want me to text him and find out?"

"I'd hoped for live music, but it sounds like this would be a good solution. It's not like I have much time to find someone else."

"Danny is good. Trust me." She texted her friend. Within moments, he texted back saying he was available.

"I'll give him your contact information and you two iron out the details. How's that?"

"That sounds great. Looks like you're saving me yet again."

She sent Danny Rick's information and sat back, satisfied another disaster had been averted.

"First you found me a way to have the party even though the pavilion was taken, now you saved the entertainment." He reached over and squeezed her hand, then left his hand covering hers.

The simple, familiar gesture of connection made her heart flutter. She didn't know why this man had such an effect on her. Of all the men in the world, her heart had chosen to fall for an actor—a complicated relationship at best. Not to mention he lived all the way across the continent.

Rick leaned over and whispered in her ear. "I want to kiss you again."

The heat of a blush rushed over her cheeks.

"I heard that." Merry laughed. "Go ahead. She could use a few kisses in her life."

## CHAPTER 13

**R**ick sat at the table at Pink Lady One the next morning, sipping his coffee, with a silly grin pulling at the corners of his mouth. He'd even managed to kiss Whitney again before she left last night, the reporters none the wiser that he'd been inside Merry's house. He'd slipped out the back door a while after Whitney had left, making sure no media was around to see him leave.

He rose and looked out the window for any sign of media around The Pink Ladies. So far, his luck had held up. That would change with his family coming to town. Soon word would be out. He reveled in his privacy while he had the chance, but at the same time guilt flooded through him that Whitney's every move was being watched.

He wandered over to the coffee pot and poured another steaming cup of the wonderful brew. The beans were from some local coffee shop and made a fine, strong, flavorful cup. He looked at the package sitting on the counter and took a quick photo of it, making a mental note to ask his assistant if she could order some whole beans of the brand and have it shipped to L.A.

Though, if he was being honest with himself, he was in such a great mood that everything probably tasted good today. Even the bowl of cereal he'd consumed... and it was just his regular pretend-to-be-kind-of-healthy brand.

He found himself humming under his breath and couldn't remember the last time he'd done that. Whistling and humming. That's what Whitney had done to him.

Life was pretty darn great right now.

The door of the rental burst open, and his sister swept inside, sucking the air out of the room, as was her wont.

Just like that, his perfect day bubble burst into a billion microscopic droplets.

His nieces, Allison and Taylor, rushed in behind his sister. "Uncle Rick." They raced over and threw themselves into his arms.

"Hey, girls." He hugged them tightly. "You're here bright and early."

"We got up before it was even light out." Taylor, the younger girl, nodded gravely.

"It was our only choice on a direct flight to Charleston. I didn't want to mess with changing planes with both the girls." Christina stood in the center of the room, taking in all the details of the rental. "Really, it would have been so much simpler if you'd had the party in Philadelphia. Or even D.C. This Indigo Bay place is just ridiculous to get to."

"Grandmere loves it here. I thought it would be a perfect place for her party."

"Did you get more help yet? I know you said you were here alone. We need a cook and some other help, of course."

He pasted on a smile while gritting his teeth. "Grandmere's cook is coming on Monday. I do have a daily staff coming to Pink Lady Two, the house next to this one. I thought you and the girls could stay there." He'd love to have his nieces here with him, but they came with baggage—his sister.

"Is there someone to bring in our bags?"

"I guess that would be me."

"We'll help, Uncle Rick." The girls rushed out the door and he followed them, escaping the look of disapproval on Christina's face, even though he wasn't sure what he'd done wrong now, except for having the party in his grandmother's favorite town.

He wasn't trying to avoid his sister, really he wasn't. He just thought the twins would like to go get some ice cream. The walk would burn off some of their extra energy. At least that was his plan. How could they still be going strong late afternoon after getting up so early?

"Uncle Rick, can I have chocolate?" Taylor skipped along on his right side.

"I want banilla." Allison tugged on his left hand.

"You can have whatever you want."

"Mom doesn't like us to have sweets before dinner." Taylor gazed up at him, concern covering her face.

"Um… we're going to eat late tonight, so it's okay." He'd told his sister he was taking the girls into town. He just hadn't mentioned to her that they were going for ice cream. Oh well. What good was being the favorite uncle if he didn't spoil them a bit?

He carefully avoided even walking on the same side of the street as Whitney's shop. Mitch was stationed outside her door and nodded at him when they walked by across the street. She was probably going nuts by now, cooped up in her shop. He hoped some new event would come along and the media would move along. As it was, he'd noticed a reduction in numbers of reporters hanging around. He guessed he wasn't such a big story after all.

He pushed open the door to The Trixie Cone, and the girls piled inside. "Hey, Rick. I see you've brought me some new customers."

"Trixie, these are my nieces, Taylor and Allison."

"How come you said Taylor's name first?" Allison looked up at him, her eyes wide. "A comes before T. I think you should say my name first."

"I… uh…" He looked at Trixie for help.

"I think your uncle probably rotates your names when he introduces you. So both of you get first billing."

Allison frowned. "Maybe. I'll have to watch him."

"You probably should." Trixie smothered a grin. "So what do you girls want?"

"Chocolate."

"Banilla."

"Okay, one chocolate cone, one *banilla*."

He wasn't even going to try to tell himself to avoid the calories. "I'll have butter pecan. Make mine a double."

He led the girls outside, and Taylor immediately dropped her cone on the sidewalk and burst into tears.

"Don't cry over spilled ice cream." He hugged her. "Come on, we'll get you another one."

They headed back inside, and Trixie made another cone for Taylor. This time the girl carefully took dainty licks of the ice cream, making sure not to topple the scoop off the cone.

There, he'd taught his niece a life lesson. His day was complete.

By the time they finished their cones, he realized there was no way Christina wouldn't know where he'd taken the girls. Taylor had a big chocolate stain on her t-shirt, and Allison had a sticky mess on her shorts that he tried to wipe off to no avail. Maybe he could sneak them into Pink Lady Two and they could go change their clothes?

Or he could just take the tongue lashing he was sure to get from his sister. He sighed and took the sticky hands of his nieces and headed back to The Pink Ladies. He even managed to not slow down as they walked past Coastal Creations—on the other side of the street, of course.

Whitney peeked out the front window of the shop and saw Rick walking down the street with two young girls at his side. Those must be his nieces. From across the street, she could still see them chattering nonstop to their uncle. Rick stopped once and bent down to tie the shoelaces of one of the girls. The other girl hung on his back while he did it. He laughed as he stood, one niece on his back, the other clutching his hand.

She smiled to herself when she saw how he was with the girls and what fun he was having. He seemed like just a normal guy, an uncle spoiling his nieces.

But he wasn't a normal guy. He was famous. There would always be people watching him.

He stood and looked toward her shop. His eyes were covered with his usual dark sunglasses and his hair hidden by a red baseball cap, but she'd know him anywhere, even in his disguise.

She stepped away from the window, wishing she

could go out there and say hi to him, meet his nieces, but she couldn't take that chance. Someone might see them. Start taking pictures again. She wanted the whole thing to go away. Well, she didn't want *him* to go away. She wanted to see him again. But she didn't know how or when that would be possible.

She headed back to the counter to set up some new displays. She couldn't concentrate on jewelry making today. Hardly any customers had come into the shop all day. She didn't know if Mitch was scaring them away, or if it was just a slow day.

She looked up at the sound of the bell over the door. Vicki Tanner swept into the shop. "Whitney, there you are."

"Here I am." Vicki had never purchased a single item from Coastal Creations, so Whitney wasn't sure why the woman was here now.

"I saw your photo in the paper. So, you and Rick Nichols. Who would ever guess he'd want to go out with you?"

She wanted to give Vicki the benefit of the doubt, that she didn't know how mean-girl she sounded, but knowing her, she meant it just the way it came out. "Did you need something, Vicki?"

"Victoria. Really, you'd think after all this time, you'd remember a simple thing like calling me Victoria. I gave up the name Vicki years ago. It's just such a... plain name. Doesn't suit me at all." *Victoria* swept her hair away from her face.

"Did you want to purchase a gift?" She made sure she had on her best may-I-help-you face.

"What? No, of course not." The woman's face held an incredulous expression. "I don't shop here. I just wondered... if you and Rick would like to come to dinner one night this week."

She sank onto the chair in disbelief. Vicki rarely spoke to her, much less invited her to her home. "I... I'm not sure what his schedule is. And I'm not really seeing him."

"He kissed you. I'd say that was seeing him."

"Well, I'm sure he's busy this week with the party for his grandmother coming up. I'm not sure when or if I'll see him again." It hurt her just to say the words because she *didn't* know when or if she'd see him again.

"Well... that's... disappointing." Vicki frowned. "If you do see him, you'll be sure to extend my invitation and call me if he says yes."

"Sure thing." *Not a chance.*

"Well, I better run." Vicki twirled around to leave. "Oh, and I can't believe you, of all people, have a security person." She left with a rustle of skirt and a slamming of the door behind her.

She rolled her eyes. What a charming person Miss Vicki-Victoria was. She doubted if Vicki would ever invite her to anything again, not that it was a great loss.

She went back to work on setting up a new display. She took out a necklace and bracelet she'd made a few weeks ago and settled it into the front of the display. She grabbed a cloth and wiped some fingerprints off the glass with more vigor than needed.

The stress and pent-up frustration from the last few days made her want to go racing to the beach, plunge straight into the surf, and swim until she could no longer move her arms.

Maybe then she'd find some peace. Maybe then she'd be too tired to think about Rick every single waking moment.

## CHAPTER 14

"Grandmere." Rick walked over and kissed his grandmother on the cheek. "You made it."

"Of course I made it, Richard." She looked around The Pink Lady and smiled. "It still looks the same. I do adore coming here. So much sunlight." She swept across the floor and stood in front of the bank of windows. "I'll never tire of this view."

"The sunsets on the bay are pretty spectacular." He walked over to stand beside her. "Did you have a good trip?"

"I did." She turned to look at him. "Everything going okay here?"

"You mean about the party?"

"I was actually asking about you and Christina. You two getting along?"

"Of course." He wasn't about to tell her about the fight he'd had with his sister last night after returning to The Pink Ladies with his ice cream-covered nieces.

"Somehow I doubt the two of you have been in the same town for twenty-four hours without a row or two."

She knew him too well. "No, everything is fine." A little white lie wouldn't hurt anything. It was Grandmere's week, and he was determined that everything was going to go smoothly.

"Now, I see there are more photos in the press of you with this Whitney we talked about. Did you invite her over for drinks like I asked? I was actually thinking maybe she'd like to come to dinner."

"Um, not yet."

"Well, I expect you to. I want to meet her. How about tomorrow night? I'll have my cook make up something for all of us. She brought an assistant with her."

Just then the twins burst through the door, letting him avoid answering his grandmother.

"Grandmere!" The twins rushed over to hug their great-grandmother.

"Well, look at you two. I swear you've grown a foot since I saw you at Christmas."

"That's 'cause we're getting older," Taylor said gravely.

Rick marveled at the differences between the girls. Taylor so serious and Allison always acting like she didn't have a care in the world. Allison drove Christina nuts, he could tell. His sister much preferred the ever-serious, ever-learning, always trying to do her absolute best so her mother would notice her, Taylor. A carbon copy of his sister like she'd been as a young girl, trying for their own mother's attention. Only, so far, Taylor was a nicer human being than his sister.

*Oops, that wasn't a very charitable thought.*

Allison drew herself up to her full height. "But I'm older than Taylor."

"You are, my dear. You'll always be twelve minutes older than Taylor."

Taylor scowled. "Yeah, I don't like that."

Rick laughed. "I'm afraid there's nothing you can do to fix that, kiddo."

She let out a sigh that was way too big for her small frame. "I guess not."

Christina followed her daughters inside, crossed over, and kissed Grandmere's cheek. "Was the trip as torturous for you as it was for me? I don't know why Rick insisted the party be here."

"Because I love it here?" Grandmere gently corrected his sister.

He smothered a grin. Grandmere didn't let Christina get away with much of her the-northeast-is-the-only-real-world nonsense. Not to mention her tendency to be a... well, a snob. Grandmere was ridiculously famous, used to fine things, and always had cooks and assistants, but she was the kindest, most down-to-earth person he'd ever met. Her employees were more friends to her than helpers. She'd never been the diva movie star.

He took a good look at her. She did look a bit

tired around the eyes. The wrinkles on her face showed a long life lived well. She'd scoffed at anyone who'd suggested plastic surgery. Though he admitted, *and not just because she was his grandmother*, the woman was gorgeous, even at eighty... or however old she actually was.

"How about I take you two to town and we'll let Grandmere unpack and your mom can have a nice break to herself."

"No more ice cream right before dinner."

Allison scowled. "Just one scoop?"

"They'll eat their vegetables, they promise." He winked at the girls.

"Really, Rick. You're just spoiling them."

"It's what favorite uncles do."

Grandmere opened her purse. "Here, girls, here's some money for your ice cream."

Just like that, the ice cream argument was settled.

"Don't forget to invite Whitney to dinner like I asked. I'd love to meet her."

"You want him to invite that local girl over?" Christina rolled her eyes. "Whatever for? He's going to mess things up with Shawna Jacobson if he keeps getting his photo taken kissing other women."

"It wasn't wo*men*, it was one woman. And there's nothing between Shawna and me."

"Well, there should be. She's a good match for you. Directors love it if the press runs with stories of the hot new couple in their movie."

"Well, that's too bad. Because we are *not* a

couple." As if his sister was ever going to think he was going to be good enough at acting, or famous enough.

"You should be. Why you'd go out with this local woman instead of Shawna is beyond me. Shawna is beautiful. Plus, dating her is good for your career."

"Such a good reason to date a woman." He wasn't sure if his sister caught his sarcasm since she was really just listening to herself, not to him.

"If you're going to have a fling, you should at least do it in private."

"Whitney is *not* a fling."

"What's a fling, Uncle Rick?" Allison asked.

"Your mother will explain that." He cocked his head and looked at his sister.

"Never mind, Allison." Christina turned away from her daughter.

Grandmere interrupted their ever-present disagreement. "If Richard likes this girl, that's good enough for me. I'd like to meet her while I'm here." She turned to him. "So you'll ask her to come?

"I'll try. I'll see if she's free." He turned to the twins.

"Come on girls. Let's go." The twins grabbed his hands, and they hurried out of the Pink Lady and into the welcoming sunshine.

"Are we going to get some ice cream even though Mom doesn't want us to?"

"You bet. Grandmere said yes. She wins."

~

Whitney hadn't seen Rick in two days now—except for the brief glance through the window. He'd called her last night, though. They'd talked for a long time, into the wee hours of the morning. She'd paid the price all day and bolstered herself with coffee throughout the afternoon.

Tonight, she'd put some peanut butter on crackers and sliced an apple for dinner. She really needed to go to the market, but that involved Mitch following her around the store, and she couldn't picture herself doing that. But she'd have to do it soon, or go out to eat... which brought with it another set of problems.

She sank onto a chair at the table and looked at her rather pathetic meal. Her phone rang, and she snatched it up, ready for the interruption.

"Hey." Rick's low, sexy voice made her smile.

"Hey, yourself." She pushed away her plate and leaned back in her chair, stretching out her legs, hoping for another long conversation.

"Did you have a good day?"

"I was kind of tired."

He laughed. "Yep, me too. It was a late night."

"It was." Though, she'd do it again tonight if he wanted. But what she *really* wanted was to see him.

"So... if I wait until after dark, how about I sneak over to your house? I'll come in the beach way."

"That would be great." Either he was reading her thoughts, or they were just in sync with each other. "I'll unlock the slider door for you."

"After we have supper here tonight, I'll escape and

come over. I could use the break from… well, I'd like to spend time with you."

"That sounds wonderful."

"I'll let Mitch know so he can keep a watch. See you soon." Rick hung up.

She got up from the table and brought the plate of food, uneaten, over to the counter. She'd go change clothes so she didn't look like such a rumpled mess from the day. She slipped on khaki shorts and a fresh shirt and padded back out to the main room. She'd sit on the couch for a few minutes to rest, then maybe, just maybe, she'd have enough energy to go back in the kitchen and finish her so-called dinner.

Rick slipped in the sliding door from the deck. He'd made sure no one was following him and knew that Whitney would have all her blinds closed, keeping out any onlookers. He slid the door closed behind him and saw Whitney sound asleep on the couch.

He quietly walked over and stood gazing down at her. A peaceful look covered her face, and her long, tanned legs stretched out on the couch. It was the most relaxed he'd seen her since this whole media mess had started. He took a step back and knocked into the coffee table. Her eyes flew open wide, and she sprang upright.

"Oh, it's you."

"It *is* me." He sat beside her. "Sorry, I didn't mean to wake you up."

"I guess I fell asleep." She adjusted her top and smoothed out her shorts. She quickly ran her fingers through her short hair, rumpling it into place, if that made any sense. But to him that seemed exactly like what she did.

She rubbed her hands over her face. "I must look a mess."

"You look adorable." He leaned over and kissed her.

She made a purring noise deep in the back of her throat that almost drove him insane. He deepened the kiss, and she wrapped an arm around his neck. "I've been wanting to do that for two days. Whose idea was it to stay away from you for so long?"

"Wasn't mine." She leaned against him and pulled him into another kiss.

He finally pulled back and looked at her, sitting beside him, her cheeks flushed. "I know we just met a little over a week ago, but... well, I like you. I have a great time with you. I feel like you spend time with me, just because I'm me. Not because of my being an actor."

"You'd be easier to be with if you *weren't* an actor." She sent him a wry smile.

"I'm sorry this has upended your life so much, but I'm not sorry I met you, that I got to know you."

"I'm not sorry for that part, either."

He held both her small hands in his, staring down

at them and her delicate wrists. Everything about this woman delighted him.

And that scared him.

A lot.

Whitney stared down at her hands, resting in Rick's. His hands were firm and muscular, strong and lean. They were perfect.

As was his smile.

And his eyes.

And just about everything about him.

*Except for that whole actor gig thing he had going on.*

She looked up into those blue eyes that changed from sky blue to stormy blue depending on his emotions. For a moment she forgot what she was going to say. "I... oh, yes. Can I get you a drink? I have a few beers or a half bottle of red wine."

"A beer sounds good."

She got up and went into the kitchen to grab two bottles of beer. She wished they could go outside and sit on the deck. It was beautiful weather tonight, but she didn't want to chance another photo of them going viral.

Especially one with him kissing her.

And she wanted him to kiss her again.

She walked over and handed him a bottle. She sat beside him on the sofa, and he draped an arm around her shoulder. So casual, so usual, and yet so foreign. Being with him was a mix of of-course-this-is-right and what-the-heck-am-I-doing.

"So, my sister is in town. And my grandmother."

"I saw you in town with the twins yesterday."

"You did?"

"I didn't think it would be a very smart idea to come out and talk to you."

"Yeah, probably not." He scowled. "It's complicated, isn't it?"

"It is."

"Anyway, Grandmere wanted me to ask you over for dinner tomorrow night. I understand if you're busy or if you don't want to be seen with me." He took a sip of his beer. "But we might be able to figure out some way for you come over, but not be seen."

"And how would that happen?"

"So you'll come if I figure something out?" His eyes turned a cobalt shade of blue. "Grandmere wants to meet you, and I like to do what makes her happy."

"I'd like to come if we can figure it out without it being another media event."

"I'll figure something out. I promise."

And she believed him. He *would* figure out a way to make it happen.

# CHAPTER 15

Late the next afternoon, Whitney glanced at the text message on her phone.

*It's all set. See you at six.*

Well, that was cryptic. Was she just supposed to walk over to The Pink Ladies? She'd noticed a photographer still lounged under a live oak tree across the street from her house. Somehow she didn't think he'd let her walk out of her house and not try to follow her.

The doorbell rang, and she went to answer the door, knowing that Mitch would have screened any visitors.

"Mere, hi."

"Hey, yourself." Merry slipped into the house wearing a large sun hat covering her hair—which was strange enough—but also a bright red wrap around her shoulders.

"I didn't know you were coming. I'm going out

tonight. I'm supposed to go to Rick's." She closed the door behind Merry.

"I know, I'm part of the plan."

"What plan?"

"The plan where I leave the house and the photographer ignores me... only it's really going to be you."

"Huh?"

"Follow along," Merry commanded. "Go put on that navy sundress you have. See, it looks a lot like this one, doesn't it?" Merry dropped her wrap and spun around. "So, you put that on, and you wear this wrap and this hat. Then you're going to sail out of the house and those silly reporters will think it's me leaving."

Whitney clapped her hands. "That's a brilliant idea."

"Don't look at me. It was Rick's. He called and asked if I'd help him set it up." Merry gave her a gentle shove. "Go get dressed. Austin will be by here about six to pick you up and take you over to The Pink Ladies."

Whitney broke into a grin. "I think this might work."

"Of course it will. Have I ever let you down?"

An hour later, after changing into her navy dress, much makeup advice from Merry, and draping the bright red wrap around her shoulders, she was ready to go.

Merry handed her the sunhat, and she settled it

on her head. With a flourish, Merry handed over a large pair of sunglasses. "No one will know it's you and not me."

Whitney hugged her friend. "You're the best."

"Make sure you tell Austin that."

They walked to the door and Merry stood to the side and called out loudly, "Bye, Merry."

Whitney grinned as she walked out the door. She got to the door of Austin's car and turned back toward the cottage. "Bye, Whitney. See you soon."

Whitney heard Austin chuckle as she slid into his car. "You and Merry make a pretty good conspiracy team."

"Thanks, Austin." Whitney opened the door of the car after they pulled up to The Pink Ladies.

"No problem. You guys have quite the subterfuge going on. Hope it works."

She swung her legs out of the car and sat, staring up at The Pink Lady. She should really get out of the car and go in…

"You okay?"

"Yes, I'm just getting up my nerve. I have to meet a bunch of Rick's family and… well, I'm not sure I'm ready."

"I can take you back to your place."

*Stop being such a coward.*

"No, I'm fine. I'm just being silly." She took a

141

deep breath, climbed out of the car, and waved as Austin pulled away. She looked up at the stairs and took a step forward. She counted each and every stair as she climbed. One. Two. Three…

The door swung open, and two young girls raced out onto the deck. "Hey, you must be Miss Layton."

"I'm Taylor." One girl slid to a stop on the top stair.

"Why do you always try and be the first to say your name?" the other identical girl asked. "I'm Allison."

Whitney climbed up the last few stairs. "Hi, glad to meet you. You can call me Whitney."

"Okay, Whitney, come inside." One of the girls —*Taylor, maybe?*—took her hand and tugged her inside.

"Uncle Rick, Uncle Rick. Whitney's here."

Rick came around the corner and smiled at her. His welcoming smile soothed her jangled nerves… well, at least a little bit.

"I see you've met the twins."

"She said we could call her Whitney," Allison—or was it Taylor—insisted. The twins hurried into the house. "Grandmere, Whitney's here."

Rick walked up and pressed a quick kiss on her cheek. She looked around to see if anyone else had seen it. He laughed at her. "It's just family."

"I'm so nervous," she whispered.

"Don't be."

"That's easy for you to say. You're not meeting a

famous actress and a surgeon and who knows who else you have here."

"You look wonderful and there is no reason to be nervous. They'll love you." He took her hand and led her into the house.

A beautiful older woman swept into the room. Whitney recognized her immediately. Viola Lemmons. She was dressed in white slacks with a precisely ironed-in crease, and a loose silk blouse. She was absolutely stunning.

The woman crossed over and took her hand. "You must be Whitney. I'm so glad you could come tonight. I'm Viola."

"N-n-nice to meet you." Had she actually stuttered?

"Richard, why don't you pour your friend a drink. You know what she likes, right? And bring me a glass of white wine. We'll go out on the deck. It's such a gorgeous night out." Viola reached for Whitney's hand, tucked it on her arm, and led her out onto the massive deck on the bay side of the house. "I love Indigo Bay summers, don't you?"

"Yes." Great, one-word answers. Viola must think she couldn't even communicate.

"Well, I do enjoy coming here in the winter, too, but summer is my favorite." Viola paused. "Or maybe spring before it gets so crowded." The woman laughed. "Okay, I like just about every season here."

Viola crossed over and gracefully slid onto a chair overlooking the bay. "Come, sit."

Whitney sat in the chair, without Viola's graceful swoop, and wished Rick would show up with their drinks. So she'd have something to do with her hands. She felt uncomfortably awkward next to this magnificent woman.

Another woman, about Rick's age, give or take, came outside and walked up to where they were sitting. "It's hot outside tonight, Grandmere. Are you sure you wouldn't rather go inside?"

"Nonsense, it's a beautiful night out. A touch of the breeze. I love the smell of the ocean air."

"I think it's humid."

The woman turned to Whitney, and she had to tell herself not to squirm under the woman's careful perusal of her. "You must be Rick's friend."

"Yes, this is Whitney. Whitney, this is Christina, my granddaughter and Rick's sister."

"Nice to meet you, Christina."

"Yes." The woman walked over to the door and called inside. "Rick, bring me a white wine, will you?"

What kind of answer was *yes* when someone said nice to meet you? Yes, Christina was glad to meet her too? Or, yes, *she* should be glad to meet Christina?

Christina settled into a chair beside her grandmother, and Rick finally came outside with a tray of drinks. He smiled at her as he handed her a beer, the same kind she'd had last time. She immediately wondered what Christina would think about her drinking a beer instead of wine like they were. Then she decided she needed to quit overanalyzing everything—as if that would ever happen.

Rick dropped into the chair beside her and took a swig of his beer. She took a dainty sip of hers, still wishing she'd asked for wine.

"So, Whitney, what is it that you do?" Christina finally said something to her.

"I own Coastal Creations, a shop in town."

"What kind of shop is it?"

"I make custom jewelry. Most of it is sea-based. Sea glass and silver. Things like that."

"Oh, so like trinkets?"

"No, not like *trinkets*, Christina." Rick glared at his sister. "Her jewelry is... well, it's like a work of art. She's very talented."

"Did you make that necklace you have on, dear?" Viola asked.

Whitney reached up to touch the red sea glass necklace that rested against her collarbone. "I did. I found this piece of glass on a trip to California. I loved the shade of it."

"It's lovely." Viola smiled. "Don't you think so, Christina?"

"Sure." Christina barely looked her direction.

"Thank you, Viola." The woman's kind remark helped lessen the sting of Christina's words and her obvious dismissal of Whitney's craft.

Rick reached over and covered her hand and squeezed it.

"So, you live here year-round?" Christina asked,

her voice skeptical.

"I do. I've lived here my whole life."

"You grew up here?"

"Yes."

"I can't imagine what a person *does* here, living here year-round. There are no good restaurants, or theater, or… well, I can see someone vacationing here to relax, *I guess*, but live here?"

Anger mixed with embarrassment coursed through her. Though what did she have to be embarrassed about? She squared her shoulders and looked straight at Christina. "I love living here in Indigo Bay. I can't imagine living anywhere else."

"Hm, that's just… so provincial."

"Knock it off, Christina." Rick's voice held a low undertone of anger.

"What? I was just saying that I can't imagine living in an area like this with none of the finer things of life. I'd be bored silly."

"Well, I think it's a lovely town. You're very lucky to live here, Whitney." Viola looked at both Rick and Christina over the top of her wine glass and gave them a that's-enough glance.

The twins came running out onto the deck, each one carrying a small tray. "Grandmere's cook said we could bring out appetizers," Taylor said. Whitney was *pretty sure* it was Taylor.

"I told you we needed more help while Grandmere is here, Richard. Look, they are even using the girls to serve food."

"Seriously, Christina. That's enough." Rick stood up and turned to one of the twins. "What do you have there?"

"These are cheese things, and Allison has some olive things."

Rick laughed. "Cheese things and olive things. My favorite appetizers."

"Can we go down in the yard and play? Uncle Rick put up a croquet set, and we want to practice."

"Stay away from the water," Christina warned.

"We will."

Rick walked over to the railing and kept an eye on the girls. "We always played croquet at family gatherings when we were growing up. Have you ever played?"

"I don't think I have."

"I'll have to show you how."

"I always thought it was a ridiculous game," Christina interjected.

"Of course you did. You're lousy at it. You like to win."

"Richard." Viola looked at him.

"Sorry."

Rick was appalled at his behavior. It was one thing to bicker with Christina when it was just the two of them, but he shouldn't let her get to him now. Not in front of Whitney. Not in front of Grandmere. But he was so angry at the way his sister was treating Whitney. She could be so impossible and always said what was on her mind. She needed an off switch. She'd be much more likable if she'd learn to keep her thoughts to herself, not that that would ever happen.

"Would you like to go down and play a game of croquet with the twins while Cook finishes making dinner?" He reached out his hand for Whitney.

He was pretty sure he saw gratitude in her eyes as she placed her hand in his and stood up.

"I'd love to."

"Let's go join the girls. Grandmere, you want to join us?"

"No, I think I'll just sit here and watch. You two have fun."

He led Whitney down the flights of stairs and out onto a flat patch of ground where the croquet was set up.

"Okay, who wants to be my partner?" Rick turned to the twins.

"I want to be Whitney's partner," Taylor said.

"How come you get to pick?" Allison glared at her twin.

"'Cause I said it first."

Rick shook his head. The twins sounded like he and Christina, which was a sad commentary on his adult relationship with his sister.

"Okay, but we're going to have to teach Whitney how to play."

"What's your favorite color? You can choose first."

Allison led the way over to the rack holding the balls and mallets.

"I'll take yellow."

Allison gave her the yellow mallet and ball. "Okay, Uncle Rick will show you how to play. He's a good teacher."

They played a round of croquet with some cheating and lots of laughter. He was pleased to see Whitney relax as they played. The girls were obviously charmed by her and went out of their way to make sure they didn't knock her ball out of the way. They had no qualms about sending his ball ricocheting out of bounds, though.

"Richard, it's time to eat," Grandmere called down from the deck.

"Coming." He turned to the girls. "Race you."

The girls squealed and ran up the stairs. He took Whitney's hand in his and they slowly climbed the stairs. "Wasn't really going to race them, I just thought something, anything might tire them out."

They climbed up to the top level. "Go on in. I'll just gather up these glasses." Rick motioned toward the door.

Whitney walked to the doorway and caught the end of Christina's conversation with Viola.

"I don't know why in the world he is going out with her when he could go out with Shawna."

Whitney froze in the doorway.

"I think Whitney is quite lovely."

"Well, she's a terrible match for Rick. He'll never get anywhere if he dates someone like her. He needs to hang out with the right people and date the right woman to assure he gets better roles."

Guilt washed over her. Christina was right. She'd only hold Rick back. It was silly to think that they could ever have a relationship. He lived his glittery life in Hollywood with the beautiful people of the movie scene. She had nothing to offer him.

Rick came up behind her. "You okay?"

"I… yes." She could barely get the words out and tried to fight back the tears that threatened the corners of her eyes. She shouldn't let Christina get to her, but she'd so wanted Rick's family to like her. She didn't think that was going to happen with Christina. Not to mention, Christina had just spelled out the truth. She wasn't a good match for Rick.

Rick frowned. "What's wrong?"

"Nothing." She silently walked into the house.

# CHAPTER 16

Last night had been a disaster as far as Rick was concerned. Whitney had been quiet all through dinner. Christina had talked about politics and Philadelphia and all the movies Viola had starred in. She'd practically been a one-woman show.

Whitney had thanked Grandmere for having her over and left after dinner, insisting she could walk home alone, which he wasn't pleased with. He'd called Mitch to be on the lookout for her.

He poured another cup of coffee and wandered over to the windows, enjoying the quiet morning, looking out over the bay.

"Richard."

He turned and smiled at his grandmother. "Good morning."

"Let me get a cup of coffee and we can go out on the deck." She poured herself a cup of coffee, added some cream, and came back beside him.

He pulled open the door, and they went outside.

"Such a nice morning. Just look at those clouds. All fluffy and white. A bit of a breeze coming from inland. I bet it changes and comes from the sea by this afternoon." She sat on the edge of a chair and took a sip of her coffee.

He sat beside her, enjoying the quiet and the view. No doubt the twins would be up soon, and any thoughts of quiet would be gone until they collapsed in a heap again tonight.

"So, this Whitney. You like her, don't you?"

"I do."

"She seems like a lovely girl."

"She is. Even if Christina doesn't think so." He couldn't help himself.

"Christina doesn't know what's best for you." His grandmother flashed a quick smile. "Even if she thinks she does."

"I know it's complicated. And I just met her. But I do have feelings for her. Feelings I've never had before, and I just feel so... comfortable with her. Like it's right being with her."

"I could see it in your eyes when you look at her. I've never seen you look at Shawna Jacobson like that. Or anyone else, for that matter."

He sighed. "It's just difficult. She doesn't like the spotlight, the media attention. She loves living here in Indigo Bay."

"You know, Richard, I married your grandfather in spite of the odds against us. I know you never knew him, but he was the love of my life. Everyone said it wouldn't last. He was all wrong for me. He was a country boy, and I was already an actress by then. But we made it work. I loved him so."

Rick looked at his grandmother. He'd never heard her talk like this.

"I've never found anyone else that I've ever wanted to be with. He had... well, he still *has*... my heart. If you care about someone, you can make it work. Just remember that, Richard."

"Our worlds are so different. I don't know that she could be happy in my world."

"Well, we sometimes have to make choices to be with the people we love." She turned to him. "You know that I'd be proud of you no matter what you do, right?"

Grandmere was always his biggest supporter, the one person he didn't have to prove himself to. Too bad it wasn't the same way with the rest of his family. He always had to prove to his family that he was worthy of their approval. "Thanks, Grandmere. That means a lot to me."

"Well, it's the truth."

Whitney took the morning coffee that Merry handed her and led her friend into the shop.

"Hey, I'm almost getting used to that Mitch guy being outside your door. At least he knows my name

153

and lets me in without asking you." Merry followed behind her to the backroom.

"Well, I'm not used to him. I don't think I'll ever get used to having a bodyguard."

Merry sat on a stool. "So, tell me all about your night at Rick's. What was his grandmother like? Is she as beautiful in person as she looks like in the movies?"

"Viola was charming. Wonderful. But, my night was... horrible." She sat across from her friend. "Just horrible. First of all, his sister is like mean-girl times twenty. She hated me."

"Well, it just matters that Rick likes you, right?"

"I don't know. Maybe that's not all that matters."

"What do you mean?"

"Well, Christina—that's his sister—along with all the nasty comments aimed at me, did say something that made sense, even if I wasn't supposed to hear it." Whitney set her coffee on the table and picked up a piece of jewelry she'd been working on.

"What did she say?"

"That I was all wrong for Rick. That he needed someone glamorous, and dating someone like Shawna Jacobson was good for his career. She said I'd only hold him back."

"That's nonsense." Merry scowled.

"But there's a hint of truth in it, isn't there? What do I know about fancy parties, movie openings, and... well, any of that stuff?" She set the necklace back down, eyeing it with a critical look, not sure what was wrong with it, but something was bothering her about it.

"But don't you think Rick can choose to date someone from that world, or can choose to date you?"

"But why are we even bothering with dating? He lives this glamorous life all the way across the country. I love it here in Indigo Bay. I hate media attention."

"There are these things called long-distance relationships, you know." Merry took a sip of her coffee. "It would be complicated, but you guys could work it out."

"What do I have to offer him, though?"

"What the heck do you mean by that? You're fabulous. He'd be lucky to have you."

"I just don't know. I would never want to hold him back in his career. I know he's always trying to prove himself to his family. No wonder Christina thinks I'm so wrong for him."

"This Christina sounds like a real peach."

Whitney looked at her phone as it lit up. Another text message from Rick.

"Aren't you going to answer him? It's him, right?"

"I don't know what to say to him."

"Don't make me do another intervention with you, Whit," Merry threatened. "I'll set up another surprise ambush if I have to. You need to talk to him. Tell him how you feel. Give him a chance. Don't run away from the best thing that's happened to you in a long time. I've seen how you look at him. You are totally smitten, and I don't think it's because he's a movie star. I think it's because you like him, the person."

"But it's complicated even to talk to him right now with the reporters hanging around."

"So what? Let him come here. Or go meet him somewhere. Let them take their pictures. You need to talk to him."

"I don't think I can take seeing more photos of me in the media."

"You're going to have to make a decision about what's important to you. A guy you obviously really like, likes you. He makes you happy. You can use all these excuses about his life in Hollywood or photos in the media, or you can choose to give this relationship a try. And I'm telling you right now, I vote for you giving it a try." Merry set down her coffee and got up. "Trust me. You'll regret it if you don't give it a chance."

She watched her friend walk away, pretty sure Merry was right, but afraid to do what she knew she needed to do.

## CHAPTER 17

"Rick, hi." She finally answered his call. Guilt was a powerful motivator.

"Whitney, I've been texting you all morning."

"I know, I'm sorry, I was… busy." She cringed, glad he couldn't see her just then."No, that's not the truth. I was avoiding you." She got up and stretched, moving away from her workbench at the shop.

"Why? Is it because of Christina? I know she was in rare form last night. I'm sorry about that."

"No… it's… listen, can we talk? I mean in person?"

"Of course. Name it, when and where?"

"You could come to my house this evening?"

"Are you sure?"

"Yes, I'm sure. We really need to talk, and I can't see that we can set up a switcheroo like we did last night every time we're going to see each other. So I'll just deal with any media attention we get."

"If you're sure, I'll be there. What time?"

"How about six? I'll make you dinner." She knew that meant Mitch was going to follow her around in the grocery store, but she was tired of the media dictating her life. She was ready to face them head-on. Or face-on. Or photo-on, however it happened.

"I'll see you then."

She set the phone on the counter and grabbed a pad of paper. What should she make for dinner? It wasn't like she was a fancy cook or anything. She needed something simple, but a recipe that wouldn't fail her. She chewed on the end of the pen and scowled. What should she make?

Rick set down his phone and smiled, ridiculously happy that he was going to see Whitney again this evening. He sat down with his to-do list and made phone calls and checked things off. Almost everything was confirmed and ready.

He played a few rounds of croquet with the twins and generally just tried to stay busy, counting the hours until six. He was dressed and ready early, and paced around the rental, waiting for it to be time to leave.

He turned as the door opened and light flooded into the entryway.

"Mother, Dad, hi. I thought you were coming tomorrow."

"A committee meeting I was supposed to go to got canceled. We caught an earlier flight." His mother crossed over and set down the small bag she was carrying. "I wasn't sure which house we were staying in."

"It doesn't matter. Your choice." Though, he kind of hoped they'd pick Pink Lady Two…

"Where are the twins staying?"

"They're staying next door."

"Ah, then, we'll stay here." His father made the decision. "It will be a bit less hectic, then."

Rick wasn't even going down the thought-road of grandparents who didn't want to be around their own grandchildren. "I'll show you to your room."

He led them upstairs to a room with a view of the bay.

"This is adequate." His mother crossed over and looked out the window. "I know Mother does love this town, though who knows why. It is quite difficult to get to."

*Christina had obviously come by her attitude genetically.*

"We could have had this in Philadelphia. There are quite nice places there to have gatherings, you know. Much easier to get to."

"But Grandmere loves this place."

"Yes, I know." His mother sighed. "And I guess we'll just have to humor her this weekend. Do you have everything set for the gala?"

"Pretty much."

"What does that mean?" His father stopped unpacking and looked over at him.

"I mean... yes, it's all set."

"That's good. You can tell us all about it at dinner tonight. I called Mother and told her we were coming early. She had Cook make a nice meal for all of us."

"Oh, I have plans tonight. I won't be here."

"Well, that is unfortunate. I thought we'd have a nice family dinner." His mother frowned. "Can you change your plans?"

"I... uh..."

His mother pinned him with her familiar disapproving look. "As we just said, this weekend is all about humoring Mother. I'm sure she'll want a family dinner."

"Okay, I'll change my plans." He didn't want to cancel on Whitney but couldn't see that he had any choice. Besides, his mother was right. The weekend was all about Grandmere.

"That's settled, then." She turned her back on him and started to unpack her suitcase. He guessed that was his dismissal.

Whitney stood at the window by the deck, looking out at the ocean. She didn't care if some creepy photographer took a photo of her. She was done with this nonsense, and she missed her views of the sea.

Besides, what did it matter? Rick wasn't coming. Oh, he'd apologized profusely for canceling at such a late moment, but he said he had to stay at The Pink Lady for a family dinner.

She could smell the aroma of a rosemary chicken baking in the oven, mixed in with the faint scent of the apple pie cooling on the counter. All that work to impress him. Even putting up with the stares of the townspeople as she hurried through the grocery store with Mitch at her side.

But Rick had more important things to do than come over to eat the meal she'd already prepared for him.

Loneliness crept over her, a feeling she wasn't used to. She'd been alone here in Indigo Bay for years. She had friends. She loved the town. She loved her life. She didn't need a man to feel whole.

Only now, one quick phone call from Rick had caused this unfamiliar feeling to descend upon her. She'd wanted to talk to him, discuss their relationship, talk to him about what Christina had said... without mentioning it was Christina who had brought up the problem.

But maybe this was some kind of sign. A sign they shouldn't talk it out. That she should just let the rest of the week play out, and then he'd been gone. She could put all this behind her and get back to normal life.

She squared her shoulders and spun around from

the window. With determined strides, she walked to the front door and threw it open. "Mitch, how about you come in and have some dinner?"

## CHAPTER 18

Rick hadn't been able to get away last night and go over to Whitney's after dinner. His family dinner had run late. His parents always thought eight at night—or later—was the proper time to eat dinner. By the time it was over and they'd questioned him on every single aspect of the party, it was too late to even call Whitney, much less go over. She couldn't keep staying up all hours of the night with him and still get up and run her business.

He set down a small suitcase as his sister, parents, and Grandmere walked in from the deck after having their morning coffee outside, though he'd heard Christina complain about how humid it was already.

"Grandmere, I have to pop out of town. I'll be back tomorrow afternoon."

"You're leaving now? Right before the party?" Christina's eyes widened, then she scowled. "It's just like you to leave after assuring us you'd deal with everything for the gala."

"I have. And I'll be back tomorrow. The party isn't until the next day. I have everything under control. I swear."

"Where are you going, dear?" Grandmere walked over and rested a hand on his arm.

"I have to fly back to New York. I have a meeting with my agent, Shawna and her agent, and the director of that new movie I was telling you about."

"Well, that's different. Of course, you should go." Christina nodded her approval. "It's important for your career. Plus, it will be good to be seen with Shawna."

"I'm not going to see Shawna. I'm going for the meeting. The director has been in London shooting a film, but now is shooting some scenes in New York and wants to meet with us while he's there." He turned to his grandmother. "But I promise I'll be back tomorrow."

"Well, it's certainly unfortunate you have to go and leave us with the preparations." His mother gave him a disapproving look. "You should learn to schedule your time better."

"Go on, Richard. We'll be fine." His grandmother touched his arm, her hand a featherweight on his wrist. "You take your meeting and we'll see you tomorrow. I'm sure you have everything under control for the party. Besides, you all shouldn't be making such a fuss over me."

He kissed his grandmother's cheek. "I love making a fuss over you."

The last thing he wanted to do right now, was to leave Indigo Bay, but he couldn't miss this opportunity to meet with the director and producer. He was pretty certain he and Shawna were going to get the leading roles, his agent had said negotiations were in the works, so he needed to go. "I'll see you all tomorrow."

He picked up his suitcase, walked out the door, and slipped into the shiny red sports car. He rolled down the windows and headed to Charleston to catch his flight. The salty air did little to erase his annoyance at this interruption to his stay in Indigo Bay. Not to mention it kept him away from Whitney for another day.

The next morning, Merry walked into the shop right as one of Whitney's customers was leaving. "Hey, I thought I'd stop by and see if you want to go to Sweet Caroline's for lunch later today."

"I don't know." Whitney reached up and rubbed her shoulders. "I still have to put the finishing touches on the jewelry set for Viola. Plus, you know, reporters."

"I thought you weren't going to let the reporters run your life? Did you get everything all talked out with Rick?"

"No, he canceled on me the other night." She shrugged. "*After* I'd made the meal. Like with twenty minutes' notice."

Merry's forehead creased. "He did? I'm kind of surprised."

"He said he had a dinner thing come up. His parents came into town early. He is here doing family stuff, so it's not like I could really complain. I understood. I was just disappointed."

"So, did you see him yesterday?"

"No, he's out of town. He called and said he was going to New York for a meeting with his agent."

"So close to the party?"

"He said he'll be back today. I plan to try to talk to him after he gets back."

Merry grabbed her phone. "Hm, let me just check... I'm going to search for the hashtag #RickNichols."

"Really? Isn't that a bit creepy?" She wasn't sure if stalking by hashtag was appropriate.

"I'm checking to see if there are any media mentions of him—*oh, shoot...*" Merry raised her eyes, looking over her phone and directly at Whitney. "I... I guess you should see this."

Merry reluctantly held out the phone to her. Whitney slowly looked at the phone, afraid of what she might see. A photo of Rick stared back at her, mocking her. A photo of Rick and *Shawna* at some fancy sidewalk cafe. The photo displayed a laughing Shawna with her hand resting on Rick's.

"Scroll, there's more."

Whitney slowly scrolled through the photos. Rick walking down some street in New York with Shawna clinging to his arm. Then, the last one, the one that did her in… Rick, holding Shawna in his arms. Not one photo of his agent. Or her agent. Just… Rick and Shawna.

Maybe it wasn't just their agents pushing them toward a relationship. Or maybe they'd decided to become a real couple. Sure looked like a real couple to her.

She handed the phone back to Merry. "I've seen enough. He lied to me, didn't he? That doesn't look like a meeting with his agent to me. He went to New York to meet up with her. He's still seeing Shawna."

"I guess maybe he is. I mean, he *is* with her, and he's holding her in that one photo."

"I've been such a fool. Worried I'm going to hold him back, that *I'm* going to hurt his career. I thought he… well, I thought he felt something for me. He said he did. I know he's an actor, but I didn't think he was acting with *me*." A dull ache flowed through her.

"I'm sorry. I guess I misread his intentions toward you, too, and I'm normally a really good judge of character. I'm sorry I ever set up that meeting with you and him at my cottage, and I'm sorry I helped you sneak over to The Pink Lady." Merry walked over and gave her a hug. "His eyes light up when he looks at you, and you seemed happy when you were with him. I guess I was just way, way off base. I didn't know he'd hurt you like this."

She pulled out of the hug and walked over to the window, staring up at the sky. "Well, at least I found out before I got in any deeper. I'm glad he didn't come over and talk the other night. It's just as well. I would look even more the fool." She whirled around to face Merry. "You know what? I'm over him. I'm over the media. I'm over having a constant security detail. I'm over all of this."

"Somehow I think it's going to take more than brave words for you to put Rick Nichols behind you."

Whitney closed the door behind Merry and crossed to the backroom to finish up the necklace for Viola. The sooner she finished, the sooner she could send it over to Rick and be done with him.

Her phone rang, and she glanced over at it, half-expecting it to be Rick. She grabbed it off the counter. "Willie, hi."

"Hey, sis. Just checking in."

All of a sudden, she needed her overprotective, always-on-her-side big brother. "It is so good to hear your voice."

"What's wrong? I can hear it. Something's wrong."

"No, I'm okay."

"And yet, you're lying to me. Spill it."

"I'm really okay. I just… well, I kind of *did* go out with Rick Nichols for a bit, but it's over now."

"The guy you kissed but insisted you weren't seeing? Ashley showed me some photos of him and Shawna Jacobson in New York. I guess he's gone from Indigo Bay, huh? Good. I didn't trust the guy."

"He's coming back to town for his grandmother's birthday party. At least I think he is." Maybe he was too tied up with Shawna in New York to come back? Would he actually miss Viola's party?

"Hope he stays away."

"Well, it doesn't matter if he comes here or stays there. I'm not seeing him again."

"I'm sorry, sis."

"Don't be. Your little sis made a fool of herself, but I'm fine. Really. I am. I'm ready to just get back to my normal life."

"I'm sorry he hurt you."

"I'd have to care about him for him to hurt me. Right now I'm just furious with him and furious with myself. But don't worry about me. I'll be fine." She said the words with as much bravado as she could muster, then hung up the phone and stared at the necklace. She *would* be fine. She'd finish the present and send it over to The Pink Lady with Mitch. There really was no reason to have Mitch hanging around anymore. She wasn't going to see Rick again. She was over him.

Totally over him.

# CHAPTER 19

Rick drove straight to Whitney's cottage from the airport. He couldn't wait to see her and didn't want to risk going to The Pink Lady first and being guilted into staying there instead of seeing Whitney. It had been three days without seeing her, and he was so over that. A few random texts back and forth. They needed to talk. This forced exile to New York had been lousy timing. He and Whitney need to talk. And not by text and not over the phone.

He pulled his car onto the crushed shell drive. He frowned when he didn't see Mitch by the door. Maybe she was still at the shop? But he hadn't seen Mitch outside Coastal Creations when he'd driven past, which made him think she was already at home.

Mitch hadn't called him like he usually did if they were headed back to her house…

*Wait.*

He snatched his phone from his pocket. He still

had his phone in airplane mode. He flipped it on and saw several texts from Mitch.

*Miss Layton insists she doesn't need me anymore.*

*She insists I leave. And I have your grandmother's present. She gave it to me to give to you.*

*Miss Layton says there is no need for my services. What do you want me to do?*

*I can't follow her if she doesn't want me to, but I'll hang around until I hear from you.*

Why had Whitney decided she no longer needed Mitch? Rick slid out of the car and crossed the distance to the door of the cottage in a few rapid strides. It didn't escape him that a reporter lounged across the street and snapped a photo of him.

"Whitney? You home?" He called through the door when she didn't answer. He grabbed his phone and dialed her number. It rang and went to voicemail. "Whitney, I'm back in town. Where are you? What's up with you sending Mitch away?"

He scowled, ended the message to Whitney, and dialed Mitch. "Mitch, what's going on? Where's Whitney?"

"She sent me packing, boss. I can't force her to use my services."

"I know that, but why did she send you away?"

"She didn't say. She just said there was no reason for me to be her security person any longer."

"I don't know what happened to make her change her mind." He looked over at the reporter and turned his back on him. "You have any idea what happened?"

"No. Her friend Merry came to see her, then left a while after that. Then Miss Layton came out and told me to leave. I hung around for a few hours across the street, waiting to hear from you. After I didn't hear back, she left the shop, came across to tell me not to follow her, and walked off."

"Okay, I'll see if I can figure it out. Don't leave town though. Let me find out what happened. Let me see if I can straighten this out."

"Sure thing."

He slid his phone back in his pocket and slowly walked to his car. He glared at the reporter taking photos of him and turned on the engine. It roared to life, and he pulled out of the drive with a spray of crushed shells.

He'd no idea where to even begin to look for her. Maybe Merry's house or Sweet Caroline's? Or maybe she was avoiding him. He *had* canceled on her at the last minute, and Christina had been really tough on her.

He pulled up to a stop sign and drummed his fingers on the steering wheel.

*Where was she?*

Whit sat at Merry's kitchen table, sipping a glass of wine. "I sent Mitch away. It's so nice to not have him following me around everywhere. Nice enough guy, but, still… I'm not really a needs-a-bodyguard type of person, am I?"

"You think Rick will argue with your decision?"

"He'd have to talk to me first, and I'm not planning on letting that happen. He made his choice when he went to go see Shawna. I'm done with him."

"If you say so." Merry looked doubtful. "But I'm totally annoyed with him right now on your behalf."

A hard rap at the front door made them both turn in unison. "I'll go get it. It's probably Austin. He said he was coming over this evening."

"I should go." Whitney started to get up.

"No, stay. He can join us for a drink."

Merry got up and went to the front room. "What are you doing here?"

"I'm looking for Whitney."

She heard Rick's voice and set down her glass abruptly, looking around the kitchen for a way to escape.

"She doesn't want to see you."

"Why not? What happened? I know I canceled dinner plans with her—"

"As if that is even a tenth of the problem," Merry accused him.

"Is she here? Let me talk to her."

"Go away." Merry slammed the door.

"Whitney, I'm going to stand here at Merry's door until you talk to me." Rick's strong, loud voice filtered through the closed door.

Merry stalked back to the kitchen. "He'll leave soon."

"I don't know. He's awfully stubborn." She pushed back from the table. "I'll go send him away myself. Tell him I don't want to talk to him. *I'm* not the one who did anything wrong. I shouldn't have to hide from him. He needs to just leave me alone."

"Or I could call the police and say I have a disturbance outside my door."

"With my luck, that would end up in the news, too. No, I'll go send him away." She got to her feet. "I'll be right back."

"You need to leave." Whitney's eyes flashed with anger as she stood in the open doorway.

"Why won't you talk to me? What happened? Are you this angry I canceled our dinner plans?"

"You mean after I'd already made dinner? No, of course not. And Mitch enjoyed your dinner very much."

"I can see you're angry. What happened?"

"Oh, maybe it's because you lied to me. Said you were going to meet your agent. Only you actually went to go see Shawna. I don't like being made a fool."

"I didn't go to see Shawna. I did meet up with my agent, and the director for the new movie, *and* Shawna's agent and her. It was a business meeting."

"That's not what it looked like in all the photos out online."

Rick frowned. "What do you mean? We went to an out-of-the-way place for the very reason I didn't want any publicity."

"Well, it appears someone saw you."

He jerked his phone out and punched up one of his social media accounts. Sure enough, there were photos of him and Shawna. He scrolled through them and scowled. Weirdly enough, there weren't any with their agents and the director. "I don't know how someone found us. It must have just been dumb luck. I told you there is nothing between Shawna and me."

"How about that photo where you're holding her in your arms?"

He looked down at his phone and searched more photos. Sure enough, there was a photo that looked like he was embracing Shawna. "I... I don't know... wait. She stumbled when we were leaving the restaurant and I caught her from falling. This has to be when this photo was taken."

"If you say so." She didn't look convinced.

"Look, there's nothing between Shawna and me. I've told you that." He took a deep breath. "If you don't trust me... well, then I guess there really isn't anything between you and me... because I can't care about someone who doesn't believe me."

"I just..." She bit her lip. "People I care about... they leave me. It's hard to trust that you won't.

Especially after seeing those photos of you and Shawna."

He looked at her, her blue eyes clouded with doubt. "I was all in on this. Ready to see where this was taking us. I haven't felt this way about someone... since, well, I don't know how long. I'm falling for you. I'm not afraid to admit that. I realize you have doubts, and I don't blame you. But I need you to trust me for this to work."

He took a step back. "I understand this is hard for you. You're afraid I'll leave you. But you're giving up, and deciding I'll leave, before you've even given us a chance. If you want to try to see where all this is heading, you let me know. And I hope you *do* want to give us a chance. But only if you can truly let yourself trust me, otherwise we have nothing."

"So did you send him packing?"

"I... he said he actually went there for a business meeting, not to meet up with Shawna. He said it was pure business."

Merry frowned. "Did you believe him?"

"I want to, but... he's an actor. Maybe he's acting with me?" Whitney sank into the chair across from her friend. "His eyes said he was telling me the truth... but, I don't know."

"I'm inclined to believe him if he says it was a business meeting with all of them. Because if he's telling the truth, then my belief in my innate sense of knowing whether a person is a good person remains intact."

"Well, we certainly don't want to blow your theory on your ultimate ability to judge people, do we?" A small grin tugged at the corners of her mouth.

"What did he say about the photo where he was holding Shawna?"

"He said she tripped and he caught her."

"Awfully coincidental that someone caught that on film." Merry bit her bottom lip. "But I guess there are always reporters looking to snap a photo of them since they've starred in so many movies together."

"He actually looked hurt that I didn't believe him. I just don't know…"

"What does your heart say?" Merry eyed her over the top of her wine glass.

"My heart says I care about him. I just need to sit down and figure out if I trust him. I need to figure out if I'm ready to take a chance with him."

## CHAPTER 20

"**W**hitney, dear. It's Viola."

Whitney set down her coffee cup, surprised to hear from Rick's grandmother. "Good morning."

"I wanted to extend you an invitation to my party tonight. You are coming, aren't you?"

"I... well, I wasn't planning to."

"I wish you would. I spoke with Richard this morning and I know things aren't... well, they are a bit rocky between you two right now. I just want to say that Richard is one of the most honest men I've ever known. And I know he cares about you. I understand if you don't want to deal with how complicated a relationship would be with Richard, but... well, I've always said that love is worth all the sacrifices."

"Viola, I—"

"You don't have to give me an answer. Just know

179

that you are welcome at my party and I'd love to see you there. You do what you feel is right for you. I wish you only the best."

"Thank you." She clicked off her phone, picked up her coffee, and walked over to the door to the deck. The sun rained down beams of light that danced off the waves. She opened the door and took a step outside, no longer thinking about reporters or photos or anything except for one thing.

Rick.

Suddenly she knew what she had to do.

Whitney took a deep swallow, squared her shoulders, and walked up to the security person outside The Pink Ladies.

"Name?"

"Whitney Layton."

The man ticked off her name from the list and smiled at her. "Have a good time."

She walked under the massive tent teeming with people. Glamorous people dressed in trendy outfits, laughing and talking. Her simple blue dress seemed plain in comparison, but she didn't care. She walked into the middle of the crowd.

"Whitney, what are you doing here?" Christina put a hand on her arm and stopped her. "I didn't know you were on the guest list."

She didn't miss the disbelief in Christina's voice.

"Viola called and asked me to come."

Christina frowned. "Well... isn't that... peculiar?" She turned and disappeared into the crowd without a word.

Whitney continued threading her way through the groups of people, not knowing one single soul but determined to continue on in her mission.

"Whitney, Whitney." The twins came rushing up to her and threw their arms around her waist. "You came to the party. Grandmere said she asked you."

"It's good to see you two." She hugged the girls, glad for friendly, familiar faces—even if they were six years old.

Taylor tugged Allison's arm. Or was it Allison tugged Taylor's arm? "Come on, Uncle Rick is over there. Let's take Whitney over to him."

The twins grabbed her hands and led her over to the far end of the tent. Rick was standing looking out at the bay, the soft breeze tossing his hair. He looked lost in thought.

"Uncle Rick, look who Taylor and I found." Allison pulled her closer to Rick.

He turned then and saw her. In spite of her good intentions, she froze, standing there looking at him like a fool.

"Hi." He only said the one word.

"Hey, Allison, let's go get some soda." Taylor tugged on her twin's hand. The twins disappeared into the crowd.

He stood there without saying another word. She

swallowed. "I... Viola invited me." She shifted uneasily on her feet. "She... I..."

She took a step closer and placed her hand on his arm. "Rick, I'm sorry I didn't believe you. I am. I think... well, I think I was afraid to believe you. Afraid to admit I care about you."

He still stood silently. The moments ticked by in slow motion. Was he going to answer her? Say anything? Her heart pounded in her chest.

"Rick, I do care about you." She looked up into his endless blue eyes. "And I trust you. Completely. I'm done running away from whatever this is between us."

"You're sure? Sure you trust me?"

"I'm positive."

Then his heart-stopping, take-her-breath-away smile spread across his face. He leaned down and kissed her. "I'm very glad to hear that. And, Whit?"

"Hm?" She wanted him to kiss her again.

"I'm falling for you. I'm actually a bit besotted by you." He reached out and touched her face.

She covered his hand with her own.

"Grandmere uses that word. Besotted. It's a great word, don't you think?" He grinned at her.

"It *is* a great word." She stood on tiptoe and kissed him.

Christina appeared beside them with a deep frown etched on her face. "Richard, I need you for a minute. Come with me. You'll excuse us?"

Rick leaned over and whispered in her ear. "I'll be right back."

She watched as Rick and his sister disappeared into the crowd.

∾

Christina stopped, and Rick practically ran into her back. "Hey." He steadied himself.

"Here he is." His sister stepped to the side.

Rick did a double-take. "What are *you* doing here?"

"What do you mean? I was on the guest list, of course." Shawna flipped her hair over her shoulder and smiled at him. Her movie star, look-at-me smile, not her genuine smile. He knew the difference. If he was right, she actually was a bit perturbed with him. He could see it in her eyes.

"I told her I'd find you." Christina had a self-satisfied look on her face.

He wanted to strangle both of them.

"My agent said I should come, of course. Yours agreed with him. We need to stop this nonsense about the local girl. It's not good for our image." Shawna threaded an arm around him, and before he could move away, a flash went off, momentarily blinding him. "I paid good money for those photos to be taken of us in New York. Let's not let them to go waste."

"You did what?"

"You didn't think it was just a coincidence, did you?"

Rick slipped out of Shawna's arm. "You know how I feel about that. I like my privacy."

"We needed the publicity. You playing around with this townie isn't helping us at all. People need to see us as a couple, an item. I couldn't let you mess up our getting this next movie."

"She's not some townie, as you put it. I like her. I like her a lot."

"Don't be ridiculous. You just met her. She's just a fling, but your timing is awful. We need to be seen together."

## CHAPTER 21

"Hello, dear."

Whitney turned at the sound of Viola's voice.

"I was hoping you'd come. I want to thank you for making this beautiful necklace. I love it." Viola ran a finger over the delicate silver wraps around the emerald green sea glass. "I love the bracelet, too. You are quite the artist."

"I'm glad you like them." She smiled at the older woman.

"You are very talented. This is so unique, and every time I wear it, it will remind me of Indigo Bay. I can't think of a more perfect gift."

"Rick helped decide on what I should make."

Viola laughed. "That's what he said, but I wasn't sure. He usually has his assistant order presents."

"He wanted to pick this out for you himself."

"Well, he did a wonderful job." Viola leaned

185

closer and whispered. "He's my favorite, not that I'd let anyone else know. He's had a hard time with his family accepting his choice in careers. He's a good actor, though."

"I think so. I admit, after I met him, I streamed about everything he's ever acted in. I know he's a star on the big screen, but my favorite of all his roles was when he had that main part in the TV drama. He was amazing."

"Ah, I think that was his best acting, too. You have a very good eye, my dear. He enjoyed doing that show. It really showed the depths of his talents. I fear he's being pegged as a romantic comedy actor now, not that there is anything wrong with that. But I don't see his eyes light up when he talks about these recent roles he's gotten." Viola gave a small shrug and touched her necklace again. "I just want him to be happy."

"Me, too." She smiled at the woman.

"Well, I guess I should go mingle with my guests." Viola swept the crowd with a look, then frowned. "Hm, I see Shawna Jacobson has come to celebrate my birthday."

She turned and searched the crowd. Sure enough, there was Shawna.

With Rick.

With her hand around his waist.

Whitney's heart did a quick flip.

"You know, dear. He really doesn't care for her. Not like that, though I do think Shawna would like him to." Viola turned and looked directly at Whitney. "I know he has feelings for you, though. He told you there is nothing between him and Shawna, didn't he?"

"He told me."

"And you believed him."

"I did. I do." She *did* believe him. She trusted him, she'd told him she did. It didn't matter what this looked like. He'd said there was nothing between him and Shawna.

"Good. He needs a woman who believes him and believes *in* him." Viola rested a hand on her arm. "I think you should go over there and introduce yourself."

"I think you're right." She covered Viola's hand with a gentle squeeze then turned and threaded her way through the crowd.

Rick glared at Shawna. She threw her head back and laughed. "Oh, I annoy you sometimes, but we get each other. We understand each other. This town girl thing will pass soon enough."

"Listen to her, Richard. She's right. She's good for you." Christina added in her two cents. Two cents he didn't need. He didn't need to be told what he thought or what he should do by either of them.

Before he knew what Shawna was doing, she reached up and kissed him on the cheek. Flashes went off. As his eyes adjusted from the flares, he saw Whitney standing directly across from them.

"Whitney... I..."

She smiled, took a step forward, and extended her hand. "Hi, you must be Shawna."

He wasn't sure who was more startled—Shawna, Christina, or him.

Shawna frowned, shook Whitney's hand, then dropped her hand to rest on his arm possessively. He reached down and disengaged himself.

"Rick has told me so much about you." Whitney stepped closer. "I'm glad to finally meet you."

Shawna looked at the photographer and shook her head no, signaling with a wave of her hand not to take any photos of the three of them. She turned back toward Whitney. "So, you're Rick's little friend here in Indigo Bay."

"Friend." Whitney laughed her sweet, melodious laugh. "I am his friend, yes. I think all couples should have their relationship based on friendship, don't you?"

He stared at Whitney in awe of her poise and grace. Not many people stood up to Shawna.

"I'm sure he's had a nice little fling with you while he was here." There was no missing Shawna's condescending tone. "Now it's time for us to get back to real life and our careers." Shawna put her hand back on his arm. Again. "Anyway, I need to steal Rick away for a bit. Our agents arranged a photo shoot on the beach. Good for publicity, you know. You don't mind, do you?"

"Actually, Rick and I were just going to grab a drink. *You* don't mind, do you?" Whitney stood her ground.

Rick threw back his head and laughed, plucked Shawna's hand off his arm, walked two strides over to Whitney, and took her in his arms. He leaned down and kissed her, her body molding into his. Lightbulbs flashed. She kissed him back, oblivious to the photographer.

She pulled away with a delightful bemused look on her face. "We're going to have our photo in the news again."

"I believe we will." He couldn't wait for the world to see how much he cared for her. He leaned over and whispered in her ear. "You're magnificent."

"You're not going with me for the photoshoot I arranged?" Shawna pouted and turned to Christina for help.

"Richard, your career needs to come first."

"Ah, but you see. That's where you are wrong. This woman right here…" He kissed Whitney again. "This woman comes first."

"You're making a big mistake." Shawna glared at him and spun around, shoving her way through the crowd.

"I will never understand you." Christina shook her head and walked away.

"I come first?" Whitney looked up at him, her eyes bright.

"You come first." He grinned at her. "And, by the way, I stand in awe of you. Not many people stand up to Shawna."

"You said there was nothing going on with her. I believed you." Her brow furrowed. "I'm not sure she does, though."

"She'll figure it out soon enough." He leaned down and kissed her one more time, grateful she was here in his arms, grateful she believed him, and super grateful he'd ever decided to have his grandmother's birthday party in Indigo Bay.

## CHAPTER 22

Rick and Whitney stood in the great room of Pink Lady One with Viola. She was surrounded by suitcases. "I'm sorry to be going. I had such a wonderful time. And Richard, you did a wonderful job planning the party and especially picking out my present. I'll cherish it always."

"Well, it's important to celebrate someone's eightieth birthday." He kissed his grandmother's cheek.

Her eyes twinkled. "I'm sure it is."

Grandmere walked over and kissed Whitney's cheek. "Goodbye, dear. It was so nice meeting you. I'm glad you and Richard seem to have worked things out. He's a good boy."

"I'm not exactly a boy anymore."

"Well, you are to someone who is… *eighty*." His grandmother smiled.

He laughed. "I love you, Grandmere."

191

"I love you, too." She turned and picked up a small bag. "Oh, and Richard, I meant to tell you. The director, Franklin DeVille—you know him, right?"

"Of course. He's very talented. He directed that drama that won all those awards last year." He respected all the man had accomplished and had followed his career closely.

"Yes, that was Franklin. He's a friend of mine and he called me. He wondered if I thought you'd be interested in a new series he's set to direct. He thinks you'd be perfect for the lead. It's a drama. I know it's not a movie, but it's a role I think you'd really enjoy. I gave him your number. He'll be calling."

"I... thank you." Surprise washed over him. How did his grandmother always know what he needed, before he even knew it himself?

"I think you should consider it. At least for a change of pace." Grandmere took a few steps, then turned and looked back over her shoulder with a grin on her wrinkled yet oh-so-beautiful face. "Oh, and did I mention the show is set in Charleston?"

He grinned. "No. That's a nice bit of information to know, though."

"Just thought you'd like to know that."

A glorious week later after spending every single day with Rick, Whitney stood on the beach in front of her cottage. The moon tossed beams of light onto the surrounding sand. Rick stood by her side, with his arm wrapped around her waist. They looked out at the endless ocean and the rolling waves caressing the shore.

"I guess I'll be able to spend a lot more time here than I thought." Rick's eyes shone. "I think I just might take that role in Franklin's TV series. He already sent me some sample scripts. It's a good role. A meaty one that will challenge me. Some will be shot on location in Charleston, some at the studio in Hollywood."

"Are you sure that's what you want?" She looked into the depths of his eyes, holding her breath, waiting for his answer.

"Would you rather I take another movie role?" A look of uncertainty flashed across his face.

"I want you to take whatever role you want. I know you'll be fabulous at whatever you do. I think you're very talented." She touched his face. "I believe in you, Richard Nicholson or Rick Nichols. I want you to do whatever makes you happy."

"*You* make me happy."

Her heart fluttered in her chest. "You make me happy, too."

Rick tilted her face up and looked directly into her eyes. "I love you."

Her heart somersaulted, and tears chased the corners of her eyes. He *loved* her. They had come so far since that day he'd walked into her shop. Being with him brought a light into her life that she'd never realized she'd been missing. At that very moment she knew, deep in her soul, how she felt about him, too. "And I love you."

Rick leaned down and kissed her gently, then wrapped his arms around her. She stood feeling his heart beat in rhythm to her own while the starlight rained down around them with a magical glow.

Read all the books and short stories in this multi-author sweet romance series set in South Carolina. The stories can be read in any order so jump in with any book!

A complete list of all the novels and stories in the series can be found here: sweetreadbooks.com/indigo-bay

NOVELS - 2018

Sweet Saturdays - Pamela Kelley

Sweet Beginnings - Melissa McClone

Sweet Starlight - Kay Correll

Sweet Forgiveness - Jean Oram

Sweet Reunion - Stacy Claflin

Sweet Entanglement - Jean C. Gordon

HOLIDAY SHORT STORIES - December 2017

Sweet Holiday Memories - Kay Correll

Sweet Holiday Wish - Melissa McClone

Sweet Holiday Surprises - Jean Oram
Sweet Holiday Traditions - Danielle Stewart

NOVELS - Summer 2017
Sweet Dreams - Stacy Claflin
Sweet Matchmaker - Jean Oram
Sweet Sunrise - Kay Correll
Sweet Illusions - Jeanette Lewis
Sweet Regrets - Jennifer Peel
Sweet Rendezvous - Danielle Stewart

Covers by Najla Qamber Designs
www.najlaqamberdesigns.com

~

The Wedding in the Grove (crossover short story between series - Josephine and Paul from The Letter.)

## LIGHTHOUSE POINT ~ THE SERIES

Wish Upon a Shell - Book One

Wedding on the Beach - Book Two

Love at the Lighthouse - Book Three

Cottage near the Point - Book Four

Return to the Island - Book Five

## INDIGO BAY ~ a multi-author series of sweet romance

Sweet Sunrise - Book Three

Sweet Holiday Memories - A short holiday story

Sweet Starlight - Book Nine

## ABOUT THE AUTHOR

Kay writes sweet, heartwarming stories that are a cross between women's fiction and contemporary romance. She is known for her charming small towns, quirky townsfolk, and enduring strong friendships between the women in her books.

Kay lives in the Midwest of the U.S. and can often be found out and about with her camera, taking a myriad of photographs which she likes to incorporate into her book covers. When not lost in her writing or photography, she can be found spending time with her ever-supportive husband, knitting, working in her garden, or playing with her puppies—two cavaliers and one naughty but adorable Australian shepherd. Kay and her husband also love to travel. When it comes to vacation time, she is torn between a nice trip to the beach or the mountains—but the mountains only get considered in the summer—she swears she's allergic to snow.

Learn more about Kay and her books at kaycorrell.com

While you're there, sign up for her newsletter to hear about new releases, sales, and giveaways.

WHERE TO FIND ME:
kaycorrell.com
authorcontact@kaycorrell.com

Join my Facebook Reader Group. We have lots of fun and you'll hear about sales and new releases first!
https://www.facebook.com/groups/KayCorrell/

Made in the USA
Lexington, KY
24 May 2018